"You're a hero."

Shay's words tore at him. Lucas Roman was no hero. Never had been. Never would be. She shivered violently and he gave up, gathering her to him.

She tipped her head back and he found himself looking into those amber eyes again. Shay's hand rose and pressed against his cheek. "You...you have to learn to accept thanks," she whispered, then stood on tiptoe and touched her lips to his.

Maybe if she hadn't smelled so good, or maybe if he hadn't felt her heat seeping into his soul, he would have stopped.

Maybe. But he didn't.

Dear Reader,

I've always been fascinated by the idea of two lost people coming together to heal each other. In *Home for a Hero*, Lucas Roman is a man who lives alone by choice. His seclusion is broken by a woman who appears on his beach and is desperately in need of his help. Although she has a busy and fulfilling job, Shay is alone, trying to figure out her life after losing her husband. Both Luke and Shay live in worlds of their own making, and it takes one spectacular moment to bring them together.

I hope you enjoy the last installment of the SHELTER ISLAND STORIES. Most of all, I hope you remember that love can appear when you least expect it—and it can change your world.

Mary Anne Wilson

HOME FOR
A HERO
Mary Anne Wilson

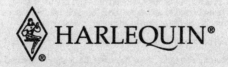

TORONTO • NEW YORK • LONDON
AMSTERDAM • PARIS • SYDNEY • HAMBURG
STOCKHOLM • ATHENS • TOKYO • MILAN • MADRID
PRAGUE • WARSAW • BUDAPEST • AUCKLAND

ISBN-13: 978-0-373-75183-9
ISBN-10:   0-373-75183-4

HOME FOR A HERO

ABOUT THE AUTHOR

Mary Anne Wilson is a Canadian transplanted to Southern California, where she lives with her husband, three children and an assortment of animals. She knew she wanted to write romances when she found herself "rewriting" the great stories in literature, such as *A Tale of Two Cities*, to give them "happy endings." Over her long career she's published more than thirty romances, had her books on bestseller lists, been nominated for Reviewer's Choice Awards and received a career nomination in romantic suspense. She's looking forward to her next thirty books.

Books by Mary Anne Wilson

HARLEQUIN AMERICAN ROMANCE

For that one person who can make love
new and real when it seems lost.
You know who you are. Thanks.

Chapter One

December 30,
Shelter Island, Washington State

Lucas Roman protected his privacy as fiercely as he'd done most everything in his thirty-seven years of life. Nothing came past the gates or over the fences that surrounded Lost Point at the farthest northern point of the island. It was his safe harbor, the only spot in the world where he could breathe easily. He was totally alone here, and it wasn't that he liked being alone—he needed the solitude to survive.

But that didn't stop him from occasionally wondering if this was what his life would be like until he ceased to exist. He only knew that right now, this was his world.

He stood at the top of the thirty-foot bluffs near the stairs cut into the rocky side that led to the hard-packed, narrow ribbon of beach below. The dense fog of early evening surrounded him and the air that filtered into his lungs was bitingly cold. He pulled his old pea coat more tightly around his six-foot two-inch frame and headed to the beach. He eased down the stairs, taking them two at a time, and jumped over the last four, landing squarely on the rock-strewn sand.

He had nowhere to go or anyplace to be. He was just killing time, walking and thinking and staying out of the house until he had no choice but to go back inside. He looked left, then right, and arbitrarily chose the right, going west. After two years of being at Lost Point on his own, he pretty much knew every nook and cranny of the land, but the beach changed regularly. Rocks and seaweed washed in with the tides, and the sand eroded, pushed and pulled both into the water and back against the rugged bluffs.

Luke felt the wind growing, and he was about to turn and go back when he saw something, a vague blur in the fog ahead of him on the beach. It was a dark misshapen pile near the water's edge. He approached, wondering if another seal had floundered on the shore, too weak to find its way into open water. But with each footstep, Luke dismissed the idea it was a seal—the object was too big, too irregular. When he got even closer, he stopped in his tracks.

He'd seen too many bodies in his life not to know that what he was looking at was human. He pulled his small flashlight out of his jacket pocket and directed the narrow beam on the body which was facedown on the sand. He hurried to get to the person, then dropped to his haunches and briefly took in the splayed arms and legs, soggy, dark jacket and equally dark hair crusted and fanned on the sand. The stranger didn't appear to be breathing.

Luke acted on instinct, doing what he'd done so often in his life. He pushed the wet hair back and found himself staring at a woman. Pressing two fingers to the artery at her throat, he was relieved when he felt a pulse.

Pulling back, he looked at a face so pale that her lashes looked as black as night. Her lips were parted, and he quickly bent toward her, putting his left hand under her neck to drop her head back, then he pinched her nose and was about to start CPR when she suddenly coughed and lurched to one side. She rolled to her right, pressing one hand to the sand and half lifting herself up as she coughed and retched.

Luke waited, knowing the best thing was to let her clear her lungs—he couldn't help her with that. He sat on his heels, watching her until she began to gulp in air and, finally, she fell weakly back onto the sand. Her eyes were closed, and she continued to struggle to breathe. Then, as he reached out to brush her hair back, her eyes flew open, looking for all the world like a waterlogged deer caught in the headlights of a car.

Her sand-caked hand lifted and she gasped, "What…what are you…?"

"Are you all right?" he asked, not making any move to get closer to her.

She exhaled, then her hand lowered to cover her

eyes. "Oh, God," she whispered as if the question had brought back whatever she'd faced in the water. Then she moved quickly, sitting up. She shook her head, then pulled her legs to her chest and pressed her face to her knees. "Oh, man," she moaned.

"What happened?" he asked.

She twisted in his direction, and her huge amber eyes narrowed. "I fell off a boat," she said, and that statement was followed by a shiver that shook her body.

There were always people in the sound—fishermen, sportsmen, visitors and commuters that traveled on the ferry from Seattle a number of times a day. "You fell off the ferry?"

"No, no," she said as she turned and pushed up to stand. She was shaky for a moment, but got her balance. Her feet were bare, and what looked like jeans clung to slender legs. Her jacket was so wet it sagged almost to her knees, and her tangle of hair stuck to her cheeks and throat. She was probably five foot six or seven and had to tip her head slightly to look up at him.

"I was…" She hugged her arms around herself and shivered again. "I was in a boat and tripped, and…" She shrugged. "I fell over the railing."

Luke took a step back without even thinking about it when she came toward him as she spoke. He knew that most islanders had given up trying to find out about the owner of Lost Point, but he had no doubt that there were reporters who still thought that finding Lucas Roman could be big news. She looked like a drowned rat, and he knew she'd been unconscious when he'd found her, but now he started to wonder just how far some people would go to get to him. He never let himself forget that people were devious and driven by what they wanted. Suddenly suspicion nudged at him; he lifted the light to her face.

"Could…you please get that light out of my eyes?"

He didn't hesitate; he'd already memorized her face. The heart-shaped face, dark eyes, sharp chin. And he saw no signs of hypothermia beyond her unsteadiness. She looked cold, but her color was good. "So, you fell off a boat and…?" he prodded.

He heard her release a shaky breath, then mutter, "Hit the water, almost drowned, got to shore and here I am."

She'd been unconscious moments ago and now she sounded almost annoyed that he was asking her anything about her presence here. "If you fell off a boat, someone must be looking for you," he said.

"I wish." She swiped at her hair again, making little leeway in getting it off her face. "I was alone on the boat, so no one knows I went overboard. At least, not yet."

Alone on a boat in the sound at night in the fog? She was either crazy or stupid. He wasn't sure which. "Okay, now what?" He knew he was being rude, but his manners had faded along with most of the remnants of his past life. He didn't care. She was up and moving around, obviously cold but breathing and in one piece. He just wanted to get her out of there.

"I need to get to a phone. My boat's out there unmanned." She took another step toward him, and this time, he stood his ground. He felt his breathing hitch. "I need to call someone and find a way to get back to the mainland."

He had a phone up at the main house, but it wasn't in service—it could call 911 in an emergency, though.

"I'll make the call for you," he said, hoping that she'd agree to stay right there while he made the call. But she didn't.

"I'll make the call myself," she said, then looked past him to the steps. "Is that the way to the phone?"

Her eyes were back on him. He didn't want her going to the house with him, but short of telling her to stay put, he didn't have much of a choice. So he gave her the only excuse he could think of at the moment. "You can't go up there barefoot. Those stones are rough and the landscape is pretty wild."

"I made it this far, so I can make it up some steps," she said without hesitation.

He gave up. Without another word, he went back to the staircase and climbed easily to the top. She was right behind him, but stepped gingerly onto the tangle of grass and ferns that had, at one time, he suspected, been a rather attractive landscape. The large trees that towered high in the dusky sky had been untrimmed for so long they almost shut out the views of the mainland across the sound and closed in the main house. The area looked wild and untamed; he liked it that way. Luke liked it more when some woman wasn't invading his world. Luke didn't want to be anyone's Good Samaritan. He didn't qualify for that on any level.

SHAY DONOVAN wasn't an impulsive person. She never had been. Measured and sure, she'd spent her twenty-eight years in a calm quietness that matched her choice of career. As a marine biologist, she studied facts. She searched and tested absolutes. Then, in one moment, one day before New Year's Eve, she acted recklessly and foolishly and ended up on a beach, half-drowned, freezing to death, with a tall stranger who had saved her.

She was cold and shaky, and her feet hurt from the rocky beach and the steps that led to the top of the towering bluffs. Fog was everywhere, blocking anything beyond five feet away from her, and the man grudgingly leading her was a mere blur in the night when she looked up at him.

"The house is over there," he said when they reached the top. He pointed off into the fog ahead of them, then took off in that direction.

She hurried to keep up, trying to avoid the errant rocks or branches that had fallen off the trees that grew with abandon all around.

"How'd you manage to get out there at this time of night and go overboard?" he asked without looking back at her.

How indeed? she thought and tried to give him a condensed version of her craziness as she followed him. "I work at the Sound Preservation Agency in Seattle, and I was doing a study on the coastline of the island. I went out to take a look around. When I left, it wasn't dark, there wasn't any fog and I didn't plan on going overboard."

He didn't respond, and she found herself adding more details to the story as they kept walking. "I took a boat that had just been serviced, but something went wrong and it died. I couldn't start it." She wouldn't tell him that today would have been her second wedding anniversary, or that she still missed Graham so much that the only way she could feel closer to him was to be on the water.

He'd loved the water. They'd met on the water, and they'd actually married on a small boat off the shore of Mexico.

She kept that to herself and added, "I contacted the coast guard, but they had a major emergency north of here, so they told me to sit tight and wait."

"Good advice," he murmured, and she felt the ground under her feet change. Stones. They were cold and damp but even. To her sore feet, they felt like silk.

She looked up and thought they must be on a terrace of sorts, and through the fog, she could barely make out the looming shadow that had to be the house.

The man led the way to the left, and gradually she could make out the rough stone and heavy timber walls that soared up two or three stories to a steeply pitched roof.

Brick steps in a sweeping half circle led up to a

heavy door, which the man opened. A light flashed on, and she found herself in a large utility room lined with cupboards on one side, shelves on the other and a very modern-looking washer and drier in an alcove.

"In here." He took her into a larger room. When he turned on the light, she was taken aback to see a kitchen that looked like something out of a turn-of-the-century hotel, with its stone walls and coved ceiling, except for the very modern appliances and slate countertops. A central island the size of a small car held a multiburner cooktop and a three-door refrigerator was directly across from where she stood and looked large enough to hold a person. Under a row of high windows on the far side of the room were three apron sinks that could have been used to bathe in if a person were desperate.

"Over there," the man said, and she glanced at a wall phone that hung in an arched nook by the refrigerator. "It's not in service, but I was told you can call 911."

She hesitated, then said, "I'm Shay Donovan by the way. Thank you so much for your help."

He nodded, then moved through a large archway to his right and out of sight. Shay shook her head. *Nice to meet you, too.* She picked up the phone, heard a dial tone and punched in 911. Once she was connected to the coast guard, she explained that she'd called earlier. They knew right away who she was, and the man on the other end of the line told her that her predicament wasn't exactly a code red—until she told him she'd fallen overboard.

"What's your status?" he asked abruptly.

She explained what had happened and that she didn't think she needed medical help.

"Thank goodness you're safe. Just wait there, and we'll do a search for the GPS signal from your craft. Give me a callback number."

"I can't. This phone isn't in service. I can call 911, but I don't think anyone can call in."

"Roger that," he said, then added. "Call us in three hours and ask for extension twenty-three."

"Thanks," she said and hung up.

When she turned her host had returned, and she got her first good look at him. She couldn't tell how old he was, maybe his early forties. She'd originally thought his hair dark, but now she could see it was a deep chestnut shot with gray. The cut was shaggy at best, combed straight back from a face that seemed to be all sharp angles where shadows cut under his jawline, at his high cheekbones and his throat.

The stubble of a new beard darkened his jaw, and a faded scar cut through his left eyebrow and across his temple to stand out against his tanned skin. He'd taken off the heavy peacoat he'd been wearing along with his boots. He stood there in his stocking feet and a plain chambray shirt with short sleeves. Dark eyes that looked almost black were narrowed on her. "What did they say?" he asked, staying in the doorway.

That I'm a fool, she thought. "They're doing a GPS tracking on the boat and asked me call them back in three hours or so." She rubbed her arms as cold water ran down her neck. "I can't believe I got myself into this mess," she said.

He shrugged as if he could believe it, even though he didn't know her, then he made an offer. "I'll drive you into town. You can find a place there to stay in until the coast guard does whatever the coast guard does."

"That would be great," she said. "How far are we from town?"

"A ways."

That was when she realized she had no idea where she'd landed when she'd managed to get to the beach. She remembered going overboard, reaching for the rope that ran along the side of the boat and missing it. Then the rip current wound around her, pulling her away from the boat, farther and farther, the fog being the only thing she could see. "Where am I?" she asked.

"On Shelter Island."

She'd figured out that one. "No I mean, I was at the northern end of the island when I went overboard, near a place called Lost Point, but by the time I was able to swim for it, I'd lost my bearings."

"You're still at the northern end," he said. "This is Lost Point."

She knew her jaw must have dropped, but managed to say, "This place, the house, that beach…?"

"Lost Point," he said.

When she'd come to the agency, they'd hired her to run tests on the waters around the island. Marine life was dying at an increasingly alarming rate, being washed up on the beaches with no obvious signs of trauma. Toxicology tests had shown nothing, so she'd been working to find an answer, with the cooperation of the islanders. They were as concerned as the agency was and had been very nice about granting access to the properties along the shore.

All but one—the owner of Lost Point and the sprawling acres on the northern tip of the island.

No amount of letters and calls to ask for access to Lost Point, a mass of rugged property on the extreme northwestern corner of the island, got any response, not even a refusal. Nothing. She'd been forced to do any work in that area from the water, and it was frustrating her, but she didn't give up trying to get access to the land, even if it was limited.

"You're about the most stubborn person I've ever met," Graham had told her. And he'd been right.

She'd dug around and tried to find out about the owner, but the name on the deed was Maurice Evans, who, it was noted, represented "the legal owner." She'd tracked down Maurice Evans to a very prestigious law firm in New York, but any calls to his offices resulted in a dead end.

One of the islanders had told her that the property had been vacant for years, then a little over two years ago, someone had bought it. No one had ever seen or met the owner, and even the crew who cleaned it once a month wasn't local.

The only person with regular access to the land was a caretaker who seldom went into town. His name was

Luke—last name unknown, and he obviously didn't answer mail for the owner. He also never answered the security buzzer Shay had tried when she'd driven to the huge gates that barred all entry to Lost Point.

Thanks to her near drowning, she had struck gold. She was not only on Lost Point, she was *in* it! "You own this property?" she asked, having a hard time seeing this man as a top-level attorney.

"No," he said. Shay was disappointed momentarily, but even though Maurice Evans was still missing, she could talk to this man. At least she thought so until he added, "Call them back and tell them I'll get you to town, to the police station if you want. I'll get my jacket and boots."

He turned before she could object. She didn't want to just leave like this. She needed time to figure out how to ask this man to get her in contact with Maurice Evans.

She heard footsteps on the stone flooring as the man returned, shrugging into his heavy jacket and wearing his boots again.

"I really appreciate all you're doing for me," she said in a rush. "I was just thinking, I have three hours before I have to call the coast guard back and I'm freezing. I hate to ask after you've been so generous with your help, but is there any way I could put my clothes in the dryer while I'm here? If I can't find a place to clean up in town, I won't be sitting there soaked to the skin."

She'd spoken quickly, afraid he'd cut her off at the

start, but she'd said everything she'd wanted and he hadn't said no. At least not yet. "What if I give you some dry clothes, then you can change. There's a Laundromat in town."

Logical, but not near what she wanted. "I guess I could, but I'm so cold." She shivered right then and it wasn't for show. The house itself didn't feel warm at all.

He stared at her hard, then said, "Okay, sure." She didn't miss the begrudging tone in his voice.

"While I'm waiting for the clothes to dry, may I take a hot shower?"

She knew she was pushing it, but she wanted to talk to him some more. He was silent for a long moment, then he countered her suggestion. "You know, if we wait around for your clothes to dry and you to take a shower, we risk everything closing in Shelter Bay. I think we need to go now."

Shay realized she'd gone too far, and chided herself, but she wouldn't lose this opportunity to find out more about Lost Point. "Please," she persisted, praying he wouldn't just tell her to get going.

He exhaled as if she exasperated him, and she probably had. She knew he wanted to say she should just be on her way, but he didn't. "Okay, but let's get going." He turned, and without another word, left the room. He didn't tell her to follow, but she did. She hurried after him, going through what had to be the most ornate dining room she'd ever seen, from the dark-wood-paneled walls to the coved ceiling that supported a huge chandelier to a table she was quite certain would seat at least twenty people.

Then they were in a two-storied great room that was separated in the middle by a stone fireplace that was empty of a fire or even logs or ashes. The room was furnished in leathers and antiques that should have been in a showroom somewhere. Few people could afford the art on the walls and she bet they were originals. She barely caught the scent of lemon oil in the chilly air before they came into a black marble entry dominated by a sweeping staircase that led to the upper levels.

He walked into a wide hallway, then turned to the right through double doors and into a large bedroom with a raised sitting area, French doors on the back wall and an arched entry to a bathroom on the left. A massive four-poster bed stood in the center of the room as if on display.

"Just get those clothes off and hand them out to me so I can get them in the dryer."

Shay slipped past him and into the bathroom and was relieved to see a sliding door on the other side of the stone arch entrance. She tugged it closed, then stopped and took a deep breath. Stripping off the soaking clothes, she cringed at the puddle that formed at her muddied feet on the polished, pale silver stones.

She piled her panties and bra on the stack, then folded her jeans, white shirt and soggy jacket around the underwear before edging the door open a crack. "Here's my clothes," she said, making sure to keep herself hidden behind the door.

"Got them," he said.

She pulled back and shut the door. She had an hour, maybe a bit more, but before she left, she was going to find the owner of Lost Point.

Chapter Two

Luke walked away with his arms full of damp clothing and hurried back to the utility room. Having Shay Donovan in his house was unsettling, but her taking a shower here…? He had to be rational about the situation, but it made him edgy. No one had been in the house since he'd arrived, except for the cleaning crew. When they arrived, he left and didn't come back until they were long gone.

He stuffed the clothing into the dryer, and dropped something. He reached down to pick up a pale pink bra, stared at it, then shook his head. He should have just driven her away from here. Now he was stuck with company for at least an hour.

Closing the dryer door, he turned it on. As the drum began to tumble, he returned to the kitchen and took time making some coffee—he could use it. He thought of Shay shaking from the cold and knew she probably could use it, too.

Luke stayed in the kitchen as long as it took to

brew the coffee, then found two mugs and poured the steaming liquid into them. God, he was acting as if he were civilized. That almost brought a wry smile to his face. Him? Civilized? He didn't think so. When he got back to the bedroom, the door to the bath was still shut. He crossed to it and knocked.

"Yes?" he heard her say faintly from within.

"There's coffee out here and a robe in there somewhere in the closet. Help yourself until your clothes dry."

He expected her to just thank him, but he didn't expect her to slide the door back enough to look out at him. He sure as hell didn't expect her to smile at him, either, or to show the dimples on either side of her full lips. She reached for the closest mug, gripped it, then said, "Thank you so much. You're really a lifesaver in more ways than one."

Then she closed the door and he was left standing there with his own coffee and wondering what he'd gotten himself into inviting her into his house.

When he'd gotten his first clear look at her, he'd felt uneasy. Tall and slender, with eyes that weren't really dark but a rich shade of amber mixed with green, she'd been so vulnerable. The freckles across her straight nose had stood out against her pale skin, and her hair—a rich chestnut shade—although soaked and matted to her temples, had started to curl at the ends. But even then, he could tell that if Shay Donovan were dry and clean and warm, she'd be a striking woman to look at.

Luke went to the great room and headed to the French doors that led out onto a secondary patio with a stunning view of the sound. He opened one of the doors, but just stood in the entry, letting the deep chill touch his face and invade the room. He had been alone so long that he'd made his own rules.

He could have dealt with finding a seal on the beach. He wasn't a people person at all, and now he just wanted this over with. He wanted Shay Donovan back in town in some trendy bed-and-breakfast, dry and safe. He didn't want her here, and he sure as hell didn't want her getting any closer.

SHAY KNEW ABOUT loneliness and being alone, but the man who had found her on the beach seemed almost empty. As she dried off, she realized he was angry, too. He hated her being here. While showering, Shay had wondered if he were the mysterious caretaker. Maybe her presence would jeopardize his job, or maybe he was working at an isolated estate because he just simply hated people, period.

She looked around the expansive bathroom, appreciating the stone walls and the large tub at the top of two steps. The doorless shower that was big enough for four people to use at once had been heavenly. She had barely noticed the bedroom, but it was just as imposing. With its stone walls and massive dark furniture made it was practically medieval, she thought with a smile. It wouldn't surprise her if there were dungeons below. That thought made her smile more.

She found the closet, a walk-in as large as most bedrooms but with few clothes in it. A couple of pairs of jeans had been folded and stacked on a side shelf, three or four chambray shirts were on hangers and a dark jacket hung in the far corner. Near the door were two white terrycloth bathrobes and she grabbed the closest one and slipped it on. It was soft and luxurious and she almost sighed. She belted it and stopped to take a look at herself in the multiple mirrors that lined the wall to the right. She wished she hadn't.

She was pale and the freckles she'd always hated stood out starkly against her skin. Her hair was a tangled mess, even though she'd done her best to finger-comb it. She turned away, wondering where the roughly dressed man who'd found her on the beach lived. Surely not in this suite or in this house. Based on what she'd seen so far, this whole estate didn't fit him. Then again, she didn't fit in here, either. Luxury and wealth weren't keystones in her life.

She turned away from the mirror and went into the bathroom, reluctant to leave the heat from the shower that lingered. But the man wanted her out of here, and she wanted to get some answers from him before he drove her into town. It wouldn't be so bad to know his name, either, she thought and smiled to herself. She padded barefoot into the bedroom area. It was dark outside and it wasn't until she glanced at her wrist that she realized her watch must have fallen off when she'd been in the water.

Her wallet! If that was gone, too, she had no money, no credit cards and no way to pay for a hotel for the night or a rental car in the morning. Her cell phone was either still on the boat or at the bottom of the sound. The soles of her feet felt tender as she headed for the bedroom door. The man had been right—the steps had been too rough for her, but she'd stubbornly insisted on climbing them anyway. Now she was paying the price.

She made her way back to the utility room, noticing more details of the house now, but seeing nothing that did away with her original impression of luxury and wealth. When she stepped into the great room, she was struck by how massive the fireplace really was as it extended to a ceiling that looked as if it belonged in some chapel or church. Painted on the stone were intricate murals that she thought had to have been done when the house had been built.

Just as she was about to leave, she stopped when she saw the man standing in front of an open door. He was staring out at the night, and the cold was seeping into the room, making it almost uncomfortably cool.

"Hello," she said. Shay knew that the man hadn't heard her at first, not until she was within about six feet of him. "I'm done," she said.

He turned quickly, and for a moment his gaze looked unfocused, then it quickly sharpened on her.

She thought she could read people, that she could pretty much tell what was going on in another person's mind, but this man gave away nothing. His eyes hid any indication of what he was feeling, and despite the crackling intensity she could sense, his face seemed oddly neutral, even when he was being abrupt with her.

It struck her that she'd seen people like this man when she'd been in therapy in the months following Graham's death. She'd reluctantly visited a psychologist and gone to group therapy for a while. A man who's name was Roy had been there. He'd come twice, then had never shown up again. This man's expression was an echo of Roy's, down to the totally unreadable eyes. Shay tried to remember why Roy had been there, but couldn't.

Unable to take the odd silence any longer, she said, "The shower was wonderful. Thanks so much."

He nodded, his usual way of responding to any thanks she gave him she realized from the short time she'd been around him.

"One more thing?" she said.

His eyes narrowed as if he were wary of what she'd ask for this time. "What?"

"Your name. You never told me your name."

There was the oddest hesitation before he finally said, "Luke."

Just Luke. At least now she knew he must be the caretaker. "Do you think you could give me the owner's address or maybe phone number so I could thank him for all you've done for me?"

He studied her, then said succinctly, "No, I can't."

"Please, I really should thank him."

He shook his head, his back still to the open door and the cold air that was getting almost unbearable for Shay. "He wouldn't expect that," he said.

"Then at least tell me what his name is?"

"It's on the mailbox," he said.

There wasn't a mailbox—she knew from her trips out here to try to talk to the owner. "If I wanted to get in touch with the owner, how could I do it?"

"Write a letter," he said and turned to the open door.

"Okay," she said softly, trying to stem her growing anger. "Then will you thank him for me?"

"Sure," he said, his back to her.

She looked away from him and turned to sit on one of the heavy leather sofas arranged in a half circle in front of the hearth. The leather was chilly, and the coldness seeped through her. "One more thing?" she said.

He turned slowly, frowning at her. "What?"

Asking him anything else about the owner clearly wasn't an option. She swallowed. "I was just wondering if we could turn on the furnace. It's so damp and—"

Before she could finish, he closed the door. "Sorry," he said.

"I didn't mean to be rude. It's just that I was noticing the art and antique collection the owner has and it seems that maybe they shouldn't be exposed to the cold and the dampness."

He looked at her as if he didn't have a clue what she was talking about, then shrugged. "Whatever."

A buzzer sounded deep in the house, and Luke moved to go past her. "Your clothes are ready," he said and headed toward the kitchen. When he came back, his arms were full, and she stood to meet him halfway across the room. He handed her the clothes that were still warm from the dryer.

"Thanks," she said, and hurried back to the bedroom and into the bathroom. She dressed quickly, relishing the heat against her skin wanting to hug it to herself. Then she felt something in her jeans pocket and pulled out her wallet. It was distorted and still very damp, but when she opened it, she found crumpled bills and her credit cards. If she only had her shoes now. She didn't remember them coming off, but she likely pushed them off when she was in the water so she could swim better.

Her jacket was still damp, but she shrugged it on over the white shirt and jeans, then hung the robe back in the closet. She headed to the great room, but when she got there Luke was nowhere in sight. She looked around, and if his jacket hadn't been lying over one of the couches, and his boots hadn't been on the floor, she would have wondered if he existed at all.

She crossed to the door he'd been standing in front of, and the fog outside was so thick it looked like a solid wall. "Luke?" she called as she opened the door and stepped out onto the flat terrace stones.

As she opened her mouth to call out again, he materialized out of the fog without a sound. "Ready to go?" he asked.

"As ready as I can be," she said and turned to go back inside.

He was right behind her, then passed her to grab his jacket. He stepped into his boots, pulled on his jacket and started back the way they'd first come into the room. "Don't you want me to close the back door?" she called after him.

"Don't bother," he said over his shoulder as he kept walking.

She went after him, through the utility room and out the open door. She stepped out and felt the slippery cold of the stones at the steps under her feet and pulled the door shut after her. The chill in the air cut right through her still-damp jacket, and she barely covered a shudder. Luke was crossing the side terrace, dissolving into the night and fog, and she hurried to catch up. She paid for it when her tender feet objected to the roughness of the stones under them, but she didn't break stride.

"Can you walk a bit slower? I don't have any shoes on and it's so dark out here, I can't see where I'm going."

Luke slowed, but didn't turn. A flashlight was suddenly in his hand and he aimed it back in her direction and on the ground. "Thanks," she said.

"Wait here," he said. "I'll get the truck." Then he was gone, taking the light with him.

She would have thought that a house like this would have at least a six-car garage and access from the house itself, but that obviously wasn't the case. She waited in the isolated darkness until she heard the faint rumble of an engine. The next thing she knew the glow of headlights cut through the fog and darkness.

The low beams caught her for a moment before they swung left and an old pickup truck slid up beside her. The passenger door opened, almost hitting her.

"Get in," Luke said from behind the wheel with his usual abruptness.

She grabbed the door and got into the cab. Sinking back in the hard seat, she let the heat that came from under the dash wrap around her sore feet.

Luke drove off, inching along, obviously seeing where he was going even if she couldn't. The next thing she knew, the massive entry gates suddenly appeared in front of them out of the fog. The truck was literally within inches of striking the barrier when it came to a shuddering stop.

She turned to Luke, expecting him to hit a remote to open the gates. He just stared at the barrier. "Do you want me to get out and open the gates?" she offered, despite not wanting to step on anything wet and cold again.

"Dammit all," Luke muttered as if she hadn't spoken.

"What?" she asked. "Do you want me to get out and help with the gates?"

She reached for the handle, but Luke stopped her when he said, "We aren't going anywhere."

"I thought you said you'd drive me into town?"

He finally turned to her, and the low glow from the dash cut odd shadows around his eyes and mouth. She'd been so thankful when he'd first found her on the beach, then excited about being in Lost Point, but now she felt a bit afraid. She remembered right then why Roy, the man in her therapy group, had been there. He'd returned from being overseas, had settled back into his life, then he'd gone to work one day and erupted over his boss's choice of coffee for the office.

She'd almost laughed at him when he'd explained it to the group. At the time, she'd been there because of her husband's sudden death, and she had been floundering in a life that had made no sense to her. Roy had been mad at his boss? Then she found out more about his background in the army and the troubles he'd had since being discharged.

Now she could see that tension in Luke, and something she should have thought about from the start came to her in a rush. She was alone with a stranger, a man she didn't know. Her stomach clenched. She made herself take a breath, calm down, and speak gently, the way the therapist had spoken to Roy. "That's okay, I can open the gate," she said. "Not a problem at all." Before she'd wanted to stay longer, but now she knew she just wanted to get into Shelter Bay.

SHAY'S OFFER WAS SIMPLE, but Luke had heard that tone before, far too many times. The don't-make-him-mad placating tone that people took when they were afraid of upsetting someone they perceived as irrational. He hated it. "We can't leave because the fog's too heavy. I almost didn't see the gates in time to stop."

"Okay." Still the tone of her voice ran over his nerves in the most unpleasant way. "Then what do you think we should do?"

Stay right here. But he didn't want that. He wanted her gone. He'd lived on Shelter Island long enough to know that driving in this fog was a stupid thing to do. If they'd left earlier, maybe he could have taken her into town before it had gotten this bad. Now there were no choices left except to stay right here…both of them. He'd learned the hard way that there were few options in this life. His last decision had been to stay where he could be found or come here. He'd chosen here, Lost Point. From then on, his options had been simple—get up in the morning or don't, live or don't.

He knew she was staring at him, waiting for something. Anything.

"What are we going to do?" she asked again patiently.

"Go back," he finally said. He'd drop her where he'd picked her up, park the truck, then figure this all out. But as he turned the wheel, she grabbed at his arm. "Wait, we can figure out—"

He didn't have any control over his reaction. He jerked away from her touch so sharply that he pulled the wheel left—hard. He braked but it was too late. He heard the squeal of tires on the wet cobbled drive, then a jerk up at the curb, followed by the truck hitting the ground with a thud.

The front end of the old truck started to sink into the muddy ground immediately. The land was so soggy from the persistent rain over the past week, the tires spun uselessly.

"We're stuck," he said, thinking that was one of the most obvious truths he'd ever stated. He grabbed the door handle to get out.

"What happened?" she asked.

He couldn't tell her that she'd caused it, that her touch had panicked him. Instead, he lied as he jumped out, "I don't know."

He took one look at the situation, then reached back into the truck to turn off the engine. "Mud up to the axles," he said without looking across at her.

"This isn't exactly a 911 incident, so I guess using the phone to call for a tow truck is out?"

"Yeah," he muttered. As out as driving her into town as soon as the fog lifted.

"Don't you have a cell phone or something?"

"No."

"Everybody has a cell phone."

"Then where's yours?" he asked, looking right at her.

She shrugged. "It…it got lost when I went overboard, but it was dead before that."

"I rest my case," he murmured.

"Well, if you don't have a working phone and there's no cell phone, what does the owner do when he—?"

"I don't know," he snapped, his nerves frayed by her constant questions about the owner.

She sank back in the seat. "Then what?"

He knew what they had to do, and he hated the thought. "We'll just have to wait until morning, then I can walk into town."

"That's an awfully long walk," she said.

He frowned at her. How did she know that? She hadn't mentioned being on the island before, but then again, he hadn't been the gracious host, either. "You've been on the island before?"

"I've been here a few times to talk to beach owners and do some studies. But even I know that it would take you a long time to get into town from here."

He'd walked the distance a couple of times when he'd needed the physical exhaustion. "I can do it," he said, and drew back, swinging the door shut after him.

Shay got out and came around to where he stood, limping slightly as she moved closer to bend over and take a look at the tires trapped in the mire. "Whoa, it really is stuck." She turned, straightening, and grimaced as she shifted her feet.

He could tell that even on the soggy ground, her feet were tender. If he'd been gallant, if he'd been more polite, he would have offered to help her, maybe even carry her so she wouldn't have to walk. But he wasn't any of those things anymore. Or maybe he hadn't forgotten good manners as he'd first thought. When she shifted again, she flinched. He flashed the light down at her feet, at the dirt and grass clinging to them, and caught a glimpse of pale pink polish on her toenails. Then he stepped toward her and picked her up.

He couldn't remember the last time he'd held a woman, but he knew that he never should have done this. Everything in him backfired. He'd thought he was doing the right thing, proving to himself that he could still be human, but the moment she was in his arms, he felt his whole being clench. She gasped and twisted to look up at him. "What are you doing?"

He wasn't at all sure himself, but he knew that he felt his whole body brace as hers leaned into his. Then her arm was around his neck, and he hurried up the driveway to the terrace and headed for the door. He pushed it open, then put her down, and backed up, unconsciously rubbing his hands together as if to free himself of that connection he'd found for a few moments. He sucked in a deep breath, then looked at Shay.

She brushed at her hair as those amber eyes lifted to him. "Thanks," she said in a soft voice.

"Sure." He turned from her, and his stomach was roiling so painfully he thought he was going to be sick. He went farther into the house without looking back, stepped out of his boots in the great room and stripped off his peacoat, tossing it over the arm of the nearest couch. When he looked back, Shay was standing across the room, far from where he stood. She was slowly taking off her jacket, but she was watching him.

She looked like a waif, pale and shaking, shifting from foot to foot again on the wooden floor, her hair wildly curling from the moisture. Luke seemed to see her so clearly at that moment that it almost made him ache. He didn't want this. He didn't want her here, and mostly, he didn't want to feel any sort of pity or concern for her. He'd passed that point in his life. He'd vowed not to care about anyone anymore, and he wasn't going to start with this woman.

He wouldn't remember her coming into this house, standing in front of him, her eyes huge, her hair clinging to her face and neck. He closed his own eyes tightly. He felt that fragmenting sensation he used to live with all the time, but had managed to push away the past few months.

"Luke?"

The sound of her voice jarred him, and his eyes opened immediately. She was still there, frowning as she came closer. That's when he moved himself, walking right past her and toward the kitchen. He reached the huge double sink, pressed his hands to the cold tile counter and swallowed hard. He knew Shay was nearby and he made himself speak without turning. "We're going to be here for a while, so I'll make some hot soup."

"That sounds blissful," Shay said, closer to him than he wanted, but still at a distance.

Blissful? Had he ever felt blissful? He decided that blissful was outside his range of emotions. He opened the cupboard by him, reached for the nearest can of soup and stared at the label until it blurred as he waited for Shay to leave. When he heard her walking away, he exhaled and was able to get air in his lungs. Blissful? No, he never had experienced bliss.

Chapter Three

By the time Luke had the soup heated, found crackers and made more coffee, he felt calmer. He put the food on a tray, then carried it into the great room. Shay was on the nearest couch, curled into one corner, her head against the pillows and her eyes closed. Her rich chestnut hair was drying into soft curls now, touching her pale skin, and her dark lashes lay in arcs on her cheeks. Her peaceful expression was almost tangible, and for a split second, he envied her. It was one thing to never know bliss, but not to have known peace for such a very long time made him ache.

He was startled when her eyes opened without warning, and her soft amber gaze was on him. She smiled, showing the dimples again. "Wonderful," she exclaimed when she saw the food and shifted to sit up straight.

He felt the impact of her expression in his middle and it was all he could do to control the urge to drop everything and walk away. He steadied himself, and went closer. After placing the tray on the end table nearest her, he returned to the kitchen for his own mug of coffee. She was holding a bowl of soup when he came back, and her content expression made his life feel grim and gray. "This is terrific," she said, and dipped her spoon in the bowl. "Really terrific."

He went to open the nearest door when she spoke again. "Luke?"

No one had said his name in this house, and now it hung in the air between them. Did Luke exist anymore? Had he ever existed?

He cautiously turned, saw her dipping a cracker into the soup, but she was looking at him. "What is it?" he asked.

"Aren't you going to eat?"

"No," he said, stepping out onto the terrace. He heard her start to say something else, but he closed the door on it. He stood in the bone-chilling cold in his stocking feet, staring into nothingness, yet couldn't get the image of Shay out of his mind. He didn't want to have her cutting through the void around him and showing him how empty his life had become. He didn't want anyone. And he didn't want her touching him again.

SHAY WATCHED the door close behind Luke, and the idea she was in any danger from the man gradually eased and dissolved. She still caught that look on Luke's face that Roy had worn during the sessions, but now, she wasn't so sure it was anger. It was more sadness. She had nothing to fear, she was sure.

Luke had shown her kindness, even if it had been grudging, offering to take her into town, drying her clothes, letting her shower, carrying her when he must have realized how sore her feet were, and now giving her the hot soup. Other than his abrupt attitude, he hadn't done a thing to make her think he might hurt her. No, she wasn't afraid of him at all. She finished the cracker and ate more soup, welcoming the heat slipping down her throat.

By the time she finished the food and sat back, Luke still hadn't come back. But as she reached for her coffee, one of the back doors opened. Luke didn't say a thing as he crossed the room and returned a few minutes later holding a steaming mug of coffee. "Do you want more?" he asked, nodding at the empty soup bowl.

"No, thanks, but it was good." She sipped a bit of her coffee, but never looked away from Luke.

He crossed to a chair over by the doors and sat down, shifting to rest his right ankle on his left knee. He tugged off his sock, tossed it on the floor by him, then took off the other one. He kept his gaze down, as if studying the steaming liquid in his cup.

"I really want to thank you for doing this for me," she said.

He glanced up, his eyes shaded by partially lowered lids. "Sure."

"You're a man of few words, aren't you?" she asked as she curled her legs under her.

"I speak when I have something to say," he murmured and took a sip of his coffee.

She was taken aback to see his hand that held the mug was unsteady. She wondered if it was from the chill outside. He didn't say anything else, but stared into the coffee. Graham had been a talker. She had always teased him that he could have had a conversation with a doorknob, but she was sure even Graham couldn't get Luke to say more than a few words.

"What do we do now?" she asked.

"Wait."

"Until?"

"The fog lifts and I walk into town."

If the fog lingered, she would have a lot of time to figure out how to make contact with Mr. Evans.

She looked away from Luke to the room they were in. "You've lived on the estate for a while?"

"A while," he echoed.

"Where did you come from?"

He rested his mug on his thigh and countered her question with his own. "Where did *you* come from?"

Okay, he was going to do it his way, and she went along with it since she was totally dependent on his generosity at the moment. And maybe if she spoke about mundane things, he'd let something slip about his boss.

"I was born in San Diego and lived there until I was eighteen. Then I moved to Houston, then Maine, spent a bit of time in San Francisco, then went back to San Diego again. Now I'm up here on a temporary assignment at the Sound Preservation Agency."

He studied her. "Thanks for that rundown and insight, but I actually meant, where did you come from *tonight?*"

She thought he was making a joke and started to smile, but he was dead serious. "I told you, I'm a marine biologist at the agency. They're having problems with the marine life dying with no apparent cause. I've done research on a bay for them at an extension near San Diego, and they asked me to visit for a couple of months to look into the problem here. Anyway, I was at work and decided to take a look up this way before I signed out for the day to check on a few things I've been uncertain about."

"Alone?"

"I was about the only one left at the office." She wouldn't mention how she realized she *was* the only one there, the only one without someone to go home to. That she was heading back to the small hotel room where she'd stayed for the past month. Or that she was having trouble getting past today, past the anniversary, and in some way, being on the water seemed to help. She'd been a fool, and she'd been reckless when she shouldn't have been.

"I didn't have anywhere to go," she said, giving a partial truth. "Then I saw the island and thought a trip over would be a good idea. I got lost in thought, and before I knew it, the fog was coming in, the motor quit and I couldn't start it."

He listened without comment now, sipped more coffee, then looked at her as if waiting for her to say something that might interest him. He wouldn't want to hear about how she'd sat on the deck of the boat, wishing Graham were there, that he'd never died, that the life she'd thought two years ago that she'd have now hadn't disappeared completely. "I called the coast guard, was waiting, turned and…I tripped. I fell over the railing and got caught in a current. I don't remember much more, until you found me on the beach."

She really was babbling now, and thankfully he spoke and stopped her. "You said you were alone on the boat?"

Very alone, she thought. "Yes. Most everyone else at the agency has been gone all week for the holidays."

"Why weren't you?" he asked, hitting the mark with his words.

She bit her lip, not at all comfortable telling this man so much about herself. Here she was, hoping to learn more about him and his boss, and she was practically spilling her life story. "I'm in Seattle temporarily, and celebrating just…" She shrugged, truly at a loss to explain how the holidays had come to mean little to her recently. "I had work to do, so I was doing it and ignoring the new year that's coming."

He sipped more coffee. "It's overrated."

"What is? Celebrating?"

"No, the concept of a new year making everything fresh."

There weren't any Christmas decorations in this space or anywhere she'd looked around the house. "So, I guess that means you ignore the holidays?"

He studied her, then said more at one time than he'd said since he'd found her on the beach. "A new year is just a new year. Nothing changes. There's no magic at midnight. It's just time passing the way it always does. People tend to make a hell of a lot more out of it than makes sense to me."

There was little emotion in his voice, yet his words made her almost shiver. She more or less agreed with him, not just at the new year, but day in and day out. Time passed. Life went on. Things didn't change. But hearing it from him filled her with a sharp sadness. "You're here alone?" she asked.

"Yes."

"No family?"

"No. How about your family? Are they here?"

She felt herself sinking back, putting an arm around her middle and pressing hard across her stomach. Family? She hadn't had family since Graham. With Luke asking her about family, it drove home that family for her didn't exist and wouldn't again. "No," she said, adopting his less-than-chatty attitude.

"No one's looking for you?"

The pain stabbed at her again. The man was suddenly making her feel more alone than she had for a long time. "No one will until someone shows up at the center, finds the boat gone and sees that I put in the security code to get the keys for it."

"When's that?"

"I guess after New Year's, maybe a day or so after."

Luke studied her and, for a moment, he frowned as his eyes flicked to the simple gold band she still wore on her left hand. "What about your husband?"

She covered the ring with her other hand and found herself biting her lip so hard she was surprised she wasn't tasting blood in her mouth. "He…" She cleared her throat. "He's gone."

Luke didn't push. She didn't have to say the words she hated, but she did, as if voicing them to this stranger would make them more real somehow. "He's dead." She looked down, easing her grip on her hand.

"Oh, I'm sorry," he said in a low voice.

She didn't want his sympathy or really to think about Graham right then, so she thanked him and changed the subject. "I wonder if the coast guard was able to find the boat."

He nodded toward another phone on the table by the tray that had held her food. "Call 911 again, and find out. Maybe you should tell them you aren't going to make it to the police tonight, either."

She reached for the receiver and once she was transferred to the coast guard, dialed extension twenty-three. Another man said they'd picked up the GPS signal from Shay's boat and they'd have it within the hour. The problem was they would have to impound the boat at their facility in Seattle for two working days. She just had to come in, show the ownership papers and pay the fees.

She hung up and muttered, "Just great," as she sank back on the couch.

"What's wrong?" Luke asked.

"They're impounding the boat when they get to it, and I'll have to pay to ransom it."

He didn't respond to that, but stood abruptly and came to collect her dishes. He took them out to the kitchen, and she heard running water, then the clank of china on china.

Money was tight, but she could manage the fines or fees or whatever they'd call them. The agency might be upset, but then again, she was a temporary employee. The worst they could do was cut short her contract and she'd go back to San Diego.

Luke came back, but didn't enter the room fully. "You can have the bed in the guest room. There's plenty of blankets in the closet."

She scrambled to her feet. "Oh, no, I can sleep on the couch, right here. No problem."

"There's no heat going—the furnace was never turned on, and it can get cold in there."

"What about a fire? I'm great at building one."

He glanced at the empty hearth, then back at her. "Not overnight."

"Where do you sleep?" she asked.

He motioned vaguely to the room they were in. "I'll be in here."

If he was going to sleep on the couch, the room

he'd offered her had to be his. "I really will be just fine on the couch," she said. "There's no reason for you to give up your bed."

He sighed. "Take it."

She almost flinched at the abruptness of his command, but decided not to fight it. "Okay, okay," she said. "Thanks." She looked around for a clock, but the only one she could see had stopped at either midnight or noon. "I lost my watch during the swim. What time is it?"

He shrugged. "I don't know, probably around ten."

"How about a television or a radio?"

"No TV. Oh, there's a television, but there's no signal. And there's probably a radio, but I'm not sure where you'd find it."

No TV, no radio. "When I get back to the mainland, I'll send you a nice TV-radio-clock combination as a thank-you gift."

"I don't have any use for them," he said.

"Everyone needs—"

"The sun comes up. The sun goes down. No need for a watch. The world does what the world does, whether I know about it or not."

"Then a nice box of chocolates it is." Lord, the man was exasperating!

With that, she left him and went to the guest room, closing the door behind her. She washed up quickly, especially her tender feet, before getting ready to slide into bed. Suddenly she realized she had only her clothes to sleep in. She slipped off her jeans, then had second thoughts about sleeping in her shirt. She had to wear it tomorrow and it was already worse for wear.

Maybe there was a T-shirt around she could wear. She looked about, ready to go and ask Luke if she could borrow something to wear, but stopped. A door slammed deep in the house, then there was no sound at all. She waited, but heard nothing. He must have gone outside again for some reason. She could wait for Luke to come back or just try to find a T-shirt on her own. She was bone-weary from everything that had happened to her and decided just to sleep in her bra and panties.

She climbed into the bed, turned off the side light, then snuggled down in the smooth sheets. She lay back, staring up at the shadows over her and marveled that she'd started her day alone in a hotel room, then alone at the agency. She'd never dreamed that she'd more or less be a castaway, washed up on Luke's beach. Now she was in his bed. Life never ceased to amaze her at its twists and turns.

If Graham had been with her he would've asked her if she'd planned on falling into the sound and getting rescued on the land she so desperately wanted to have access to. She would've laughed and told him that was his way of doing things. He hadn't been a man who saw limits on what he could do. If it meant protecting something or someone, or finding the truth, all rules were off. But she'd never been that bold. Or maybe that crazy. Was that was why she'd been so attracted to Graham at first?

She was startled to realize that the memories of her husband were coming softly now, slipping into her mind. She remembered falling in love with Graham. They'd met when Graham had been hired as a guest lecturer on marine studies at the university in San Diego where she'd been working as a department assistant. She'd heard his lecture and later had approached him. They had coffee, talked some more and before she knew it, they'd become good friends.

Then the love had come, sneaking up on her. At the thought of how she'd loved him, her stomach clenched, and she rolled onto her side, the sensations as familiar to her as the sense of loss that never seemed to leave her since Graham's death. At the beginning she had tried to fight the emotions, hoping to make them go away. But they'd never stopped completely, and after a time, she'd given up. She'd learned to let the feelings come and leave on their own.

But for the first time, the aching loss of her husband was dissolving almost as soon as it began. She shifted and felt for the slim gold band on her finger, rubbing the smooth metal the way she had for so long. But rather than looking for comfort, she was almost scared to think things were changing.

If the pain went away, did that mean she'd forget Graham? She wasn't sure that was a deal she wanted to make, exchanging the pain for forgetfulness. She didn't ever want not to remember Graham. But the pain was easing and that sense of loss she'd lived with for two years was less defined. She suddenly found herself having to concentrate to conjure up Graham's image.

She wanted to remember the way his gray eyes had narrowed with intense interest on everything from his charts and maps to the way a soft-serve ice cream swirled in its cone. To remember his rusty hair that was always too long and mussed from him constantly running his hands over it when he was deep in thought. His long fingers rapping on the desktop when he spoke on the phone. He hated the business end of his career in marine biology. He loved spending time on the water, the discoveries he'd make, and he'd loved her.

But it had been for such a short time—barely seven months. One minute he'd been telling her that he'd been invited on a lecture tour in Europe, and they could take a side trip to visit a preservation park on the African shore. The next moment he'd keeled over. There'd been no warning, no clues of the aneurysm. He was gone before she could even reach for him. She'd held on to him until they'd forced her to let him go.

Now, when she thought about him, his image blurred and was undefined as if a mist were falling between them. She couldn't see the details and started to panic. As she pushed herself up in the bed, a loud knocking on the bedroom door startled her. "Y-yes?" she managed to say around a tightness in her throat.

"Sorry, I need to get a few things," Luke said through the wooden barrier.

"Oh, sure, of course," she called. "Just a minute." She got out of bed, turned on the side light, grabbed her shirt and pulled it on, then pushed her legs into her jeans. As she zipped them, she padded barefoot to the door.

She stood to one side to let Luke in. "Just be a minute," he murmured as he made his way to the dresser. He opened a middle drawer, took out some socks and then reached to the far side of the large dresser and picked up something that looked like a sleeping bag. When he turned, she saw that his chambray shirt was open and untucked. She caught a glimpse of a strong, smooth chest and a flat stomach before her eyes jerked up to his face. She felt herself blush, and was embarrassed by where her thoughts had started to go.

Her stomach flipped, but for an entirely different reason this time. How could she be looking at this stranger with anything but polite interest, especially right now? She clasped her hands together in front of her, feeling the cool metal of her ring.

"I hope I didn't wake you," he said, flicking his eyes over her jeans and shirt.

"I wasn't sleeping," she said, keeping her eyes determinedly on his face.

"Well, then, good night." He pulled the door shut behind him.

She hurried to undress and got back into bed before turning off the light and pulling the blankets over her. She took several deep breaths, blocking out what had just happened, then finally closed her eyes. She just wanted to sleep—she was bone-tired—but couldn't.

The minute she shut her eyes, she could see Luke on the shore, a blurred figure in the fog and night. Then the man who had just left the room, his feet bare, his shirt undone, his chest naked, took his place. She tried to push the image away, but found she couldn't. She missed feeling warmth at her back, arms around her.

Suddenly she heard a thud from another part of the house, then silence.

She rolled on her side, thinking about Luke's isolation, and she realized she was just as isolated, only not on an island but in a crowded world.

Closing her eyes more tightly, Shay told herself she was safe and warm here. She wasn't in the water—or worse. Finally she let herself fall into the coming sleep, past dreams that flitted in and out of her consciousness but made little sense.

"No! Don't!"

Shay was jarred from a deep sleep by muffled screams. At least she thought that was what had awakened her. "No, stop! Dammit, stop!"

Chapter Four

Shay sat up in the darkness and listened. It sounded as if Luke was yelling at someone. His voice was muffled by the door, but loud enough for her to understand most of the words. "I can't do it again!"

Was he talking to the owner? Had Maurice Evans come to the house somehow? Or was it friend of Luke's? Were they having an argument?

The words were lower, unintelligible now, but the tone was the same—stressed, almost panicked. She hesitated, then got out of bed into the cold air of the room. She grabbed her clothes and got them on as she crossed to the door. Opening it a crack, she almost jumped back when Luke screamed, "Not again! Not again! I won't!" The words vibrated through the house.

"No!"

She heard raw, pained fear in the single word and she opened the door farther to look out into the hallway. Right then, a door slammed—hard. She stepped out onto the cold marble floor and slowly walked in the direction of the voices that were quieter now.

She entered the great room, the voice low, almost a sob now. "Please, no, please." She glanced around quickly, but couldn't see anyone. A low light was on by the couch, but Luke was nowhere in sight. As far as she could tell, no other person was there. She heard a muffled cry, then another.

She almost retreated back to the bedroom to lock the door, but another sob pulled her forward. It was guttural and filled with agony. She felt the deep chill in the room at the same moment she saw one of the back doors was open. She walked silently toward it, listening, but the voices had stopped. The bedroll was tangled on the floor in front of the doors, and just as she was about to step over it to look outside, she stopped. Something moved to her right, and she looked into shadows alongside the doors and saw Luke. He was hunched over, his head on his knees, his image blurred in the faint light. He was shaking. Shay hesitated, then moved closer, crouching down next to him. "Luke? Luke?" she said softly.

He exhaled, then lifted his face to her. His hand flew out, capturing her wrist. It startled her, but she stayed where she was. "You," he breathed hoarsely, as if shocked that it was her talking to him and not someone else.

THE MAN IN BLACK was coming toward Luke. No face, no sounds. Approaching him slowly, getting closer, then standing over him, questioning. The voice was low, above a whisper. "Tell me everything. Now."

Luke tried to get up, to get away, but he couldn't move. His arms and legs were pinned to the wooden floor with chains and the rope around his neck tightened if he dared move his head even an inch. "Tell me," the man floating over him demanded again. "Now!"

Luke saw it all. He tried to blot out the horror, but he felt it all, and the screams filling the room were his own. He begged, pleaded, but nothing stopped what was happening. The pain came in a rush, stronger and stronger, and he struggled in a futile attempt to stop it. He finally could move his hands and push to his feet. He wanted to run, but his feet were still chained. His heart felt as if it was going to burst out of his chest. He heard his name and the screams drifted away. He looked up, reached out and he saw Shay sitting next to him, pity in her eyes.

"Luke, it's me, Shay," she said in that tone he'd heard when they'd tried to drive to town. "You…you were screaming."

The screams? He shook his head, trying to rid himself of the remnants of the nightmare, but it stayed with him. It had been months—six or seven—since he'd had an episode. He'd almost forgotten—until now.

He slowly drew back, then pushed to his feet as Shay followed suit. He raked his fingers through his hair, then brushed his hands roughly over his face, barely able to look at the woman in front of him. He pushed his shaking hands into his jeans pockets.

Leaning back, he let the closed door support him for a moment while he caught his breath and tried to focus. "Pick a spot and focus on it," his doctor at the hospital had told him. But all Luke could see was Shay.

She bit her lip, and he hated the pity in her eyes. He wanted to wipe it away, but couldn't think of one way to do that. "You were arguing, talking to… someone, and I thought…"

Oh, God, he'd been talking? She'd heard him begging, pleading, screaming? He closed his eyes tightly, then as he opened them, his mind fragmented even more. Words caught in his throat. Nothing would come out. No apology, no explanation.

Shay took a step toward him, holding one hand out to him. He twisted away, moving to the side, to the open door, and took one last look at her.

"I'm sorry," he said, then went out into the foggy night. He moved quickly along the terrace, through the coldness.

"Luke?"

His name echoed behind him, but he kept going, away from Shay and away from the images that bombarded him. He didn't stop until he was at the small guest house that hugged the top of the bluffs. Walking around the back, he went up onto a deck that faced the view of the mainland. But he could see little now, just fog and emptiness.

He should have slept out here. He should have put distance between himself and Shay. Going to the upper floor wouldn't have been good enough. He didn't like being confined there, but he could have been fine out here. When he was alone, the dreams didn't matter.

Shay had looked so delicate when she'd found him, with her hair tousled around her pale face. And those eyes. Even in the blur after the nightmare, her concern for him had been very clear.

He headed to the back door of the small house, which he'd had kept up, too. Luke hadn't cared about either house being clean, but Maurice had insisted they were an investment and worth the money and effort.

Luke tried the door and it opened right away. He entered the main room, a tenth the size of the great room at the main house. The air was thick and it was completely dark inside. The smell was the same as in the main house, heavy with lemon oil. He flicked on an overhead light and saw the sparsely furnished space. A couch, a chair, a table. A tiny kitchen was off to his right, and a single bedroom and bath to his left. It was as plain and sterile as the main house was plush and overdone. It would do for him.

He slowly sank down to the floor, sitting cross-legged, and considered just staying here until morning. But he knew leaving the way he had would've made Shay uneasy. He'd have to go back and explain things to her, then come out here to sleep after. No, he'd stay here until it was almost dawn, *then* he'd go back. He didn't want to face her just yet, and he hoped that she'd gone back to bed.

Closing his eyes, he tried to concentrate on breathing. That was a mistake.

Images flashed in his mind; a long hallway, bare ceiling lights, the echo of booted feet on stone floors. Beaten wooden doors were set in walls thick enough to hide or muffle anything going on in the tiny rooms off the corridor. But Luke could hear everything—the screams, the shouting. He pressed his hands over his ears and pulled his knees to his chest.

"Breathe," he told himself. "Just breathe and don't stop. Focus. Focus." He waited and waited until he finally felt that moment when he could push himself past the memories, past the shadows of fear, and he exhaled in a trembling rush. He slowly leaned forward and pushed himself to his feet. He didn't know what time it was when he finally left the guest house.

Leaving the light on, he headed out the back and toward the main house. The fog was so thick he could barely see his hand in front of his face, but he welcomed the dark isolation and the biting cold. Light always made him feel exposed and he hated that. Heat suffocated him. He got to the still-open French door, went inside and stopped.

Thankfully Shay wasn't there. His relief was overwhelming. She'd probably gone back to bed, and he could just stay here until it was light, then walk into town. Shay could leave tomorrow, and if he could figure out how, he'd explain just a bit about his behavior. Just enough for her not to pity him.

He looked for paper and a pen, then scrawled a

note for Shay, letting her know where he was going. He walked to the guest room and stopped at the closed door. He heard nothing, then folded the note and slipped it under the door. She'd find it in the morning after he'd left.

Turning to leave, he took one look behind him, then headed to the guest house where he sank down on the couch.

He knew he wouldn't sleep. He didn't want to dream again. He didn't want to relive the moment the man in black came for him, and he didn't want Shay to ever see him like that again.

Never.

SHAY WOKE WITH A START. Thin gray light filled the room and rain beat down on the roof and against the walls. She stretched and the chill in the air raised goose bumps on her bare arms. She was tempted just to pull the blankets back over her, then remembered Luke and his dream.

A nightmare. People had them, but she'd never seen a person who appeared so overcome by what he'd dreamed. Lines had been etched deeply at the corners of his mouth, and his eyes had been narrowed, barely meeting her gaze. She'd waited for what seemed forever for him to come back, but finally knew that he wasn't going to return, at least not while she was waiting for him.

She'd finally gone back to her bedroom and hadn't hesitate turning the lock before she crawled into bed.

She'd lain in the dark waiting for sounds that told her Luke had come home, but when she'd finally slipped into sleep, she'd known she was still alone.

She pulled off the blankets, got up and padded barefoot to the door, stopping just short of pressing her ear to it. She couldn't hear anything except the rain outside. Cautiously she opened the door just enough peek out into the hallway. She couldn't see Luke, but saw something flutter to the floor out of the corner of her eye.

She picked up a folded sheet of paper off the black marble. "Luke?"

There was no response. She stepped back, closed the door, then opened the paper. "Gone to town. Back soon." The note was signed *L*.

She quickly got dressed, finger-combed her hair and tucked it back behind her ears. She avoided looking in the mirror before she rushed to the great room. The doors were all closed now, but sheeting rain obscured most of the view beyond.

If Luke had walked into town in this downpour, she doubted he'd get back anytime soon, if at all. She turned and the emptiness in the house was almost palpable. Hugging her arms around herself, she went back toward the kitchen, which was as empty as the rest of the house.

Uncertain of what to do next, she noticed the side door was ajar. Maybe the wind had blown it open, or Luke had forgotten to close it when he left. She crossed to it and looked out. The rain was coming down so hard and driven so fiercely by the wind it sprayed into the house. She quickly closed the door and retreated to the kitchen, where she spotted the coffeemaker, its light glowing red.

The idea of hot coffee was appealing this chilly morning, but when she picked up the carafe, she saw the liquid was dark and sluggish, obviously left over from the previous night. She tried to find fresh coffee, opening one cabinet after the other until she came across a good-sized pantry with just about every dried, canned or bottled food a person could need. She found a sealed bag of ground coffee and in a matter of minutes had the maker going.

She poured a mug of the steaming liquid, cradled it in both hands and wished the air in the room was as warm as the ceramic she was holding. Leaning back against the counter, she sipped the coffee and let it warm her.

Luke must have walked to town after all. She knew it had be four or five miles. With a glance at the windows over the large apron sinks, she shook her head. What would possess him to go out in that?

He was probably embarrassed, but he shouldn't be. She'd had horrible dreams herself and could sympathize. After Graham died, she'd had few peaceful nights. She didn't understand what Luke's dreams had been about, but she'd clearly seen the pain in his eyes.

She sipped her coffee and wandered through the chilly house, wishing she had some shoes or socks to protect her feet from the cold marble underfoot.

Although Shay couldn't begin to understand what was going on with Luke, his leaving gave her the perfect opportunity to explore. With luck, she'd find out who the mysterious owner of Lost Point was.

She went up the staircase, found at least seven bedrooms and as many baths. None were furnished, except for what she thought was the master bedroom. It had an even larger version of the bed she'd slept in last night, situated dead in the middle of the medieval-looking room. The bed was stripped, and there were no personal belongings anywhere in sight.

She headed back downstairs and stepped into a sitting room on the bottom floor, before finding a small library stacked with books she'd guess were probably first editions. Continuing down a short hallway, she turned into a solarium where rain streaked the glass walls and ceiling. Grayness was everywhere and not a plant brightened the space.

Farther down the hallway, she walked into what must be a media room. A huge TV was built into the side wall, along with more components then she could count. She crossed the floor and turned on the TV, but got nothing but static.

Sighing, she flipped it off, then spotted a very low-tech item that made her smile. A radio. It was in direct contrast to the other devices in the room, set at the back of a low shelf, and when she reached for it, dust covered her fingertips.

She quickly turned on the power button, heard static, turned the dial, and found an oldies station she listened to on the mainland. Strains of a Sam Cooke song filtered into the room.

She quickly unplugged her treasure and took it back to the great room. Setting it on the hearth, she plugged it into a nearby socket and turned up the volume. Sooner or later, there would be a newsbreak or a weather report. She took her now-empty mug out to the kitchen, poured more coffee, then found bread and a toaster. She made herself two slices, put peanut butter on them, and nibbled on her makeshift breakfast.

She glanced at a clock on the wall, but it had stopped. She wished she knew what time it was, then she saw a digital readout on the stove. The low green glow read one-fifteen.

Goodness, she'd slept awfully late, and if Luke had left first thing this morning, he'd been gone four or five hours. He might have already reached town by now.

She took her coffee with her to the bedroom. Her feet were cold, and she was ready to put on her jacket, which she'd hung in the closet off the bathroom last night so it would dry completely. As she tugged her jacket off its wooden hanger, the dark coat in the corner caught her eye again. She shrugged into her jacket and pulled the coat from the closet. It was dark navy, and felt like heavy wool to her. She lifted the sleeve and realized it was a uniform jacket, maybe from the navy, she didn't know for sure, but there were gold bars on it. They went halfway to the elbow, and another one was on the front. A light coating of dust was on the shoulders, as if the coat hadn't been worn in a long time.

She let the fabric fall from her fingers then stepped back and closed the door. Did it belong to Luke? Had he been in some branch of the service? Maybe an officer? She had a hard time seeing his beard-roughened face and longer hair belonging to someone in the military. Then again, she'd met a man who'd been in the air force, and as soon as he'd been discharged, he'd dyed his hair blue and cut it into a Mohawk. Rebellion against the rules at its best, she'd thought back then.

She returned to the great room and sat on the couch, tucking her cold feet under her, listening to the music and waiting for some newscast to cut in and maybe verify the time. Luke's opinion that sunrise and sunset were fine tellers of time didn't wash with her. It was past noon, but with no sun and the driving rain, Shay wasn't entirely sure the clock on the stove was accurate.

Finally the DJ interrupted the music with a spiel for a car dealership in Seattle, then a weather report.

"This is promising to be one of the worst storms to hit the Seattle-Tacoma area in years. There are three fronts hanging out over the Pacific, with colder air and promising even more rain."

Finally, he said, "And now, at one-thirty, I've got an oldie and a real goody for all you lovers on New Year's Eve day. 'What Are You Doing New Year's Eve?'" The music started and the strains of the ballad filled the spaces around her.

Shay felt her throat suddenly tighten, and she swiped at eyes that burned with tears as it hit her that she had no idea what she was going to do this New Year's or the next or the next for the rest of her life.

She stood quickly, quelling the flood of self-pity and went back to the kitchen to warm up her coffee. Where could Luke be?

"Where's that music coming from?"

Shay gasped. As if she'd conjured him up just thinking of him, Luke spoke from behind her. Turning, she saw him standing in the doorway to the utility room. He was in a dark poncho with a hood he brushed back off his head. Water was dripping everywhere around him.

"Don't you ever warn someone when you sneak up on them?" she asked a bit breathlessly.

"I'll signal you next time," he said as he toed out of his muddy boots. "Where's the music coming from?" he repeated.

"A radio I found in a room with a huge TV. Trouble is it only gets an oldies station clearly, but they have weather and news every ten minutes or so."

He shrugged out of his poncho and reached back to put it in the utility room. In the kitchen, he eyed her coffee and she found herself offering to get him a cup as if she were the hostess and he was the guest.

"I could use it," he said. She found another cup, poured coffee into it and handed it to him. "The walk into town didn't happen, not with this storm." He took a sip before he added, "So we'll be here for a while. You can stay in the bedroom here and I'll go down to the guest house near the bluffs."

She'd doubted he could make it into town in a storm like the one beating down on them, but she hadn't expected him to say he was moving. "What are you talking about? Where've you been if you couldn't get into town?"

"Never made it there, so you're here for a few days."

"That part I get," she admitted. "And I'm grateful for the place to stay, believe me, very grateful. But why do you have to go to the guest house? There are seven bedrooms upstairs, and I could just move to one of them, then you can have your room back."

"I'll be fine at the guest house," he said before he sipped more coffee.

"That doesn't make sense."

He pinned her with an intense look that made her breath catch in her chest. "After last night, I think we'd both sleep better if I wasn't in the house."

She shook her head as she remembered the pain in his eyes. "You had a nightmare. Everyone has nightmares."

"Sure," he said, but his tone said he didn't agree with her.

"I have them. It's nothing unusual."

He motioned to the other part of the house. "Come on. We have to talk." If she hadn't stopped him, he would have taken off, leaving her to follow him.

"Luke, it's cold in here. Why don't you let me put on a fire."

He put his mug down, and went back to the utility room. She heard things being moved, and when she got to the doorway, she saw Luke had opened a door set in the side wall. From where she stood, she could see the small side room had a slanted roof, rock walls and a large wood bin filled to the top with cut logs. Luke got an armload, and she moved back to let him through. Following him, she picked up his half-full mug of coffee on the way.

He laid the wood on the hearth, then crouched to place logs in the firebox. Soon, a fire glowed and before long, the wood was crackling and snapping.

He stood, turned to Shay and motioned to one of the couches. "Sit down."

She didn't move.

"Please," he said.

She crossed to the couch and as soon as she sat, Luke pulled an overstuffed chair closer. She took her jacket off when the heat from the growing fire touched her, and she laid it next to her. Luke pressed his hands flat on his thighs and took a breath that made his shoulders shake. "Okay, I have to…" He exhaled harshly, shook his head, and she could see the tips of his fingers go white as he pressed them into the denim of his legs. "I need to explain. One time. That's it. No questions."

He'd set down the rules and she knew instinctively that she couldn't negotiate any of the terms. "Okay," she said quickly, clasping her hands in her lap, not at all sure she really wanted to know what his nightmare had been about.

He lowered his head, and she could see him close

his eyes for a long moment. "I was in a situation before that wasn't easy. It affected a lot of what I do, and how I react now. Hell, it affects everything now." His voice was flat and he stared hard at his hands.

"I live alone on purpose, so I don't involve anyone else in my problems. I haven't had the nightmares for a long time, but they're still there. And you're here." That's when he looked up, and eyes that hadn't given away a lot up to that point, gave away everything. There was a bleakness in them that was difficult for Shay to look at. "You don't have any part in what my life is, at least, not beyond sitting out this storm. And the nightmares are for me to deal with alone."

She didn't understand. "They're just dreams—"

She barely got the words out before he said, "Sure they are."

She studied his face, not sure what to say now. There was a barrier between them, and she couldn't read his expression. But she knew the nightmares were more than just bad dreams to him. Or maybe he was just embarrassed, as she'd thought originally.

"You know, it's really nothing. You didn't say anything wrong last night, and there's no reason to be upset about it."

"Sure." She hated it when he said that word. He wasn't all right with the situation. That was one thing she was sure of herself.

"Okay, okay," she murmured, and offered him a compromise. She didn't want to be in this house by herself, and something in her hated the idea of him being so alone when he had his nightmares. "I'll keep the door closed, and when I'm sleeping, if I hear anything, I won't come out" She glanced at the fire, enjoying the wave of heat spreading toward her. "The DJ said more storms are coming. It will be nice and cozy in here with the fire going."

His expression grew tight, lines etching deeply at the corners of his mouth and at his eyes. "Cozy?" She thought he was going to laugh at her choice of words, but there was no humor in his voice. "I don't think so."

"Okay, how about warm and dry?" she said quickly.

His eyes held hers for a long moment before he looked down at his hands, which had curled into fists on his thighs. "We'll talk about this later," he said only a bit louder than a whisper.

She'd take that. That gave her time. "I know you want to be alone, and I promise you, when I can get out of here, I will."

He rose and turned away from her, going to the French doors and staring out at the storm that was battering the house. "I don't do well around other people. I'm used to having things my way, and my way isn't always the way others would have things."

"Such as?" she asked.

"I like leaving the doors open. I'm claustrophobic. I can barely stand being inside," he said.

Whatever drove him to open doors and go out in the cold without a jacket or boots seemed a far cry from having simple claustrophobia. But she didn't challenge him. "Then open the door."

He sighed heavily. "This can't work."

She stared at his back. "Let's just try it tonight and if it…if it's not good, then I guess the guest house would be an answer."

He sighed heavily, turned and slanted a dark look at her. "Okay. For tonight."

She bit back her automatic thank you and simply said, "For tonight."

Chapter Five

Luke stood, pushing the chair back with his legs as he straightened. "I'll go get more wood," he said.

Shay was looking up at him as if she wanted to say more, but thankfully she didn't. He'd meant it when he said no questions. He had no answers she would want to hear. Pressing his hands flat on the cold glass of the door, he watched the storm raging outside.

"While you do that, do you mind if I look around the kitchen for something to make a meal out of? An early dinner?"

"Do whatever you want for yourself. I don't expect you to cook for me."

"I'm not a great cook, but I can microwave with the best of them, and I saw that there's a pretty nice-looking microwave oven in the kitchen. If I'm getting myself something, it's no bother to make you something, too. Besides, as I said, I really do owe you more than a hot meal."

He could see her reflection in the rain-streaked glass

as she watched him. Her expression was blurry, and he was okay with that. "You don't owe me anything."

"I sure do," she insisted. "What do you like to eat?"

Not interested in arguing further who owed whom, he accepted her offer. "Anything's fine."

"I thought I could make something nice." She shrugged. "I know neither one of us buys into this New Year's Eve thing, but a nice dinner wouldn't be all bad." She stopped and even in the hazy reflection he could see she was biting her lip. "I mean, it's not a celebration or anything. Just food."

"Whatever," he said.

"Is there any wine or beer?"

He focused on the rainy day. A fully stocked wine cellar had come with the house with brandies and even some exceptional cognac. It was really too bad that he'd used some of the collection to just get drunk, but he hadn't been down there for months. "Off the kitchen there's some stairs. The door at the bottom is where you'll find the wine cellar. Help yourself. There isn't any beer."

"Okay, wine sounds lovely. It goes with anything."

He didn't doubt it would, but he didn't want to stand there making small talk. He rubbed his chilly hands together. "You know, I'm going to take a look at the furnace. It might just need to be turned on."

"That would be great. If you can get the heat going, I'll make an especially nice dinner."

"It's a deal," he muttered and crossed the room to go toward the entry.

"The furnace isn't in the basement?" she asked, and he waved off her question.

"The main system is, but there's one near the solarium. I'll try it first," he explained and kept walking.

It had been a long shot, but twenty minutes later he'd managed to turn on the heater from the auxiliary. The pipes rattled as air whooshed through, then he could feel the heat starting. As soon as Shay left, he'd shut the furnace down again.

Back in the house, Luke got to the entry off the dining room and stopped. Shay was at the sink, washing large brown potatoes. On a tray on the counter sat two steaks, obviously defrosting, and a pan that held a loaf of bread.

"Heat's on," he said, and she jumped at the sound of his voice.

He watched her lift her face to the ceiling in surprise, then she smiled. Those dimples came from nowhere and her eyes brightened, startling him.

"I can feel it." Then those amber eyes met his. "You are a miracle worker."

God, he couldn't stand her smiling *and* complimenting him, too. "Just a switch and a dial," he muttered before adding something he hadn't been aware he was going to say until the words were out. "I've been thinking. I'll stay in the main house, but you have to tell me if you want me to leave. Okay?"

SHAY COULDN'T BELIEVE IT. He'd backed down. She spoke up quickly and without thinking about her actions went closer and held out her hand to him. "Deal. I'll let you know if I want you to leave." She said the words, but knew there were few things that would drive her to tell him to go. Very few.

With a nod, Luke left the kitchen, and Shay turned back to the meal with a grin on her face. She wouldn't be alone. She liked that idea. More than she dared to admit. "I'll let you know when the food's ready," she called out without looking back.

"Great."

The music played while she worked, and by the time she was ready to put on the steaks, it was getting darker out. The last time given on the radio had been three-thirty. While the pan heated on the stove, she went to the great room.

Between the fire in the hearth and the furnace, the air was beginning to warm and the air blowing through the vents had quieted. She could barely hear it over the beating rain and wind. "How do you like your steak?" she asked Luke who was by the back doors.

"Rare."

She started to go back to the kitchen, but stopped when she saw him stoop to pick up the bedroll and a pillow. For a moment she thought he'd changed his mind and he was leaving after all. "What are you doing?" she asked.

His dark eyes met hers. "I'm just putting this stuff behind the couch for later."

"Oh, okay, sure," she said, relieved. "When I go to bed, you can have the doors open all you want."

He dropped the bedroll and pillow to the floor. "I said I'm not going unless you tell me to. You don't have to bribe me to stay."

She really must be transparent. "It wasn't a bribe," she said, recognizing the lie when it came out. "I just know that with the heat going you might not be too comfortable with being closed in and all."

"I'll manage," he said, his face tightened.

"I'll be gone before you know," she added. "Then you can get back to your own life. I know you want to be alone."

That didn't do a thing to soften the look on his face. If anything, it deepened the lines around his mouth. "Yeah, my life," he breathed. "Being alone takes a lot of work."

That was her life, too. And she was startled by the urge she had to comfort Luke, to let him know that everyone had their demons. Everyone had ghosts that haunted them. "I understand," she said softly.

He turned back to the door, placing his palms against the glass. His shoulders hunched forward as he pressed the top of his head to the window. "Sure you do," he said, and she knew he'd actually said there was no way she could.

"Luke, I told you I didn't have family waiting for me, or worrying about me. I should have explained that my husband…he's dead." There, she'd said it again. Suddenly a thought came to her out of the blue. "Did you lose someone?" If he'd lost a spouse as she had, she could truly empathize with what he was going through. Maybe she could offer him some solace.

She waited for a very long time before he turned slowly, his expression bleak. "Yeah, myself," he said.

SHAY STOOD A DISTANCE from Luke, her hands clasped tightly in front of her, and her eyes… It was her eyes that got him. They had the same pity in them as they'd had when she'd found him last night. He didn't want her pity or anyone else's.

"I need to go and close up the guest house," he heard himself saying as he crossed into the kitchen. The music seemed to be everywhere, grating on his nerves, and the warmer it got in the house, the harder it was for him to breathe. He heard Shay behind him as he went to get his poncho and step into his boots.

As he opened the door she called after him, "You're coming back, aren't you?"

He nodded and plunged out into the rain. He ran as if being pursued and he didn't slow until he was at the back deck door and in the small house. Stopping in the middle of the living area, he couldn't begin to understand why he'd offered to stay at the big house. All he knew was, he'd looked at Shay and seen the disappointment on her face when he'd said he was leaving, a part of him wanted to see her smile. He'd stay only until she told him to go. Or, he amended silently to himself, when he himself knew it was time to go.

He glanced around and thought he should have

moved out here in the beginning instead of camping in the main house. The guest building was small, spare and close to the water and the deck wouldn't have been too bad to sleep on when he needed to. To maintain his privacy, he could have altered the cleaning crew's duties, limiting them to the main house. He'd never have had to see them, or have to leave while they did their job.

Luke stayed in the guest house for a while, just sitting on the couch, gazing out the open back door. Rain splattered on the floor, but he didn't move to close the door. He just sat there watching. Finally, he got up. He'd eat a meal with Shay, then he'd sleep on the bedroll in the great room. And maybe this time, he wouldn't dream. The man in black would be gone, and Luke could have a bit of peace.

Once outside, he closed the door and took several deep breaths before heading to the deck stairs. He didn't care that the hood on his poncho had fallen back and his hair and face were getting soaked. He jogged onto the lawn and toward the house, but as he got closer, he slowed to a walk. He hesitated at the door, then went inside.

The radio was still on, playing some doo-wop music, and Shay was in the kitchen, working at the stove. Steam rose into the air, and he could smell something spicy. She glanced up at him, her face flushed and she smiled. She seemed relieved that he'd actually come back, but it certainly made her look achingly lovely.

He looked away from her as he took off his poncho and boots, then grabbed a towel out of a cupboard over the washing machine and rubbed at his hair. After finally tossing the towel onto the dryer, he turned and said, "It smells good."

"I was going to do baked potatoes, but decided on potatoes au gratin when I found some nice cheese. We have peas, some crusty bread that I found in the freezer and the steaks."

"Gourmet," he murmured. The music in the great room was driving him nuts, and he was about to turn it off when an emergency weather report cut into the programming. A second weather front was approaching them, and more rain and high winds were expected.

"It's not letting up, is it?" Shay asked.

He glanced at her. She was carrying plates and silverware. "I totally didn't think about a table, and the one in the dining room is so huge," she said.

"I'll get one," he said. When he left the great room, he could feel cold water running down his back from his trip out in the rain, and he needed another towel. Making his way to the guest suite bathroom, he deliberately didn't look at the big bed still mussed from Shay sleeping in it.

He grabbed the first towel he saw and rubbed his hair vigorously. Sure it was now dry, he raked his hair back from his face and got a fresh shirt out of the closet. After he changed, he went to get a card table from a hall closet and took it into the great room.

Shay had left the plates and silverware on the

hearth by the radio, and he set up the table between the couch and the chair he'd moved earlier. Then he started setting the table.

When Shay returned, she was carrying a bottle of wine and two glasses. "That wine cellar is wonderful. I'm no expert, but I got a pinot noir, and it's really good." She put the glasses on the table, poured wine into both and motioned to Luke to take one. "Help yourself," she said. "And remind me to thank your boss for the wine."

Carrying his glass, Luke sat down on the hearth, and rested the goblet on his thigh. He knew that any man confined to a room with an attractive woman on a rainy day with wine and music would have a line or at least an opening gambit to get some small talk going. But he drew a blank. His conversational skills hadn't only been damaged while he'd been held hostage in Iraq, but after his ordeal, he'd become used to weighing every word. Eventually, it became easier just to keep quiet.

Now he didn't know what to say to Shay, so when she came back with a tray holding a plate with two steaks on it, a small dish with cheese and potatoes and a bowl of peas, he kept his mouth shut. He guessed that the bread was what was wrapped in a hand towel on the side of the tray.

She put everything down on the table, then said, "I'll be right back," and hurried out of the room again.

When she returned, she had her wineglass in her hand. After taking a sip, she motioned to the table. "Everything's ready."

She took the seat on the couch, crossing her legs yoga-style and he noticed the pale pink toenail polish again. It suited her somehow and he almost smiled. When was the last time he'd smiled? He drank some of his wine as he sat down in the chair opposite Shay, and welcomed the heat of the alcohol sliding down his throat.

"How long have you been living here?" she asked as she put her goblet down on the table.

That he could answer. "Two years."

"Help yourself while it's hot."

He used a fork to get a steak onto his plate, some potatoes and the peas. Shay did the same, then pulled back the towel and offered him a piece of bread.

He took it but didn't eat anything at first. His hands were less than steady, and he didn't know why. Then he had a thought that this was the first time he'd eaten with anyone since he'd come to Lost Point. Ridiculous but true.

He looked at Shay, who popped a piece of steak into her mouth and glanced up at him as she chewed. For the past two years he'd eaten every meal either standing or sitting on the deck. Sometimes he didn't even remember to eat. Now he was looking at food that could qualify as a feast, yet he couldn't make himself pick up his fork to spear some of it and put it in his mouth.

Shay set her fork down with a clatter on her plate, and sat back. "Is there something wrong with the food?"

"Oh, I…" He picked up his fork, amazed his hand was fairly steady now. "I was just appreciating the fact that this is a real meal."

She chuckled softly. "As opposed to an unreal one?"

Unable to meet her smile, he stared at his food. "As opposed to eating out of a can," he said, and got a forkful of potatoes.

"Oh, you poor man," she murmured. "Please, enjoy a no-can meal with my blessing."

Suddenly his nerves eased, thanks to her soft laughter and her smile. He tasted the potatoes, then the steak. He almost sighed with pleasure, but caught himself before he did. "This is good."

"A man who's easy to please," she said.

"In some ways." He was amazed at how normal the conversation was becoming. "How about you? Are you high-maintenance or easy?"

"Probably high-maintenance. Graham used to say I could agree on one thing, then the next minute I wouldn't."

"Graham?"

Her sunny disposition was gone with wrenching speed. "My husband."

Luke nodded and looked away from the sadness that filled her eyes now. The sorrow he saw was heartbreaking. "Oh," was all he said. He bent over his food, concentrating on getting peas on his fork. He finally mashed them with the tines and shoved them into his mouth.

He looked up at Shay, saw her take a breath that

made her shoulders tremble, then she exhaled and straightened. She tried to smile, but it never reached her eyes.

"I told you, I'm not good at holidays. They just seem so empty," he said.

She held up a hand. "I'm sorry. I guess the storm and things just…" She shook her head. "I'm not usually maudlin. Graham used to say things go on and work out no matter what happens, and he was right." She slowly lowered her hand to her side. "They do work out. I've got a great job and I get to travel and I love what I do. I've wanted to swim with dolphins for forever and now I get to do that sometimes and when I don't, I'm still around the water."

He could almost see her mind turning from the past and trying to look to the future. He envied her. The past was a weight on him, always there, and he couldn't avoid it. He'd sighed, and as he thought about Shay leaving, he was struck by the fact that his future looked as empty as anything he'd ever seen.

He drained the last of his wine, then stood and turned away from Shay. His first thought was flight. It always was and he hated that reaction to run instead of dealing with his problems and working them through. This time he made himself not open the door.

"Luke?"

He closed his eyes tightly at the sound of his name. Then he took a breath, calmed his nerves and faced her. "Sorry," he said, because there was nothing else to say. "Checking on the storm." That was ridiculous, but the words served to protect himself somehow.

"The radio said the storm is going to keep up for a while," she replied.

The night was being torn apart by wind and rain, yet words could do the same thing to him, just a look could. Dammit, he'd never thought he was a vulnerable man. He'd thought he was strong enough to get through anything. But right then, he wasn't so sure.

"Your food's going to get cold," Shay said.

Polite words. Simple manners. *Say thanks and sit down.* He didn't thank her, he did sit down again. He reached for his knife and fork, and cut up more steak. He ate potatoes and peas and ripped his bread.

And he could have kept doing it if Shay hadn't said, "Is it too hot in here for you?"

"No, it's fine." He shoved some steak into his mouth.

Shay reached for the wine bottle and poured them both another glass, then she sat back and ate quietly. He watched her while she finished the last of her dinner, and noticed her hands. Long, slender fingers, plain nails, and the thin gold band. Her husband was dead, but she still wore the ring. How long had she said her husband had been gone? He couldn't remember if she'd told him, but his name had been Graham.

She caught him staring at her and sat back with a sigh. She lifted her eyes to the ceiling where the rain thundered against the roof. "I really love having a fire," she said.

He didn't look at the fireplace. The room had

been getting hotter and hotter and he was on the verge of turning off the heater. "You're warm enough?" he asked.

"Yes, I'm fine. It's just so nice on a day like this to have a fire crackling in the hearth."

He pushed back from the table and took his wine-glass with him as he went to look outside. Heat was a discomfort for him, but a comfort to most normal people. He'd set the thermostat to sixty-five, but it felt like ninety now. He saw Shay's reflection in the glass, and their eyes met. "I wonder what your boss will say when he finds out I've been here and raided his wine cellar?"

"He won't care," Luke said and looked out at the world growing darker by the moment. He drank more wine. "It's just wine and a house."

"Some house," she said.

Suddenly the music cut off and the news came on. "Another storm is coming off the Pacific, and it's predicted to bring even more rain and thunderheads, along with an extreme drop in temperature."

Luke watched rain wash down the glass on the door. "More rain," he grumbled.

"I guess you'll have a guest longer than we thought," she whispered.

Part of Luke wanted her gone, but another part, one he hadn't known had survived in him, wanted her to stay. That bothered him almost as much as what had happened last night.

Shaking off the memories, he helped Shay clean

up. Afterward, she sat on the couch in the great room, and he laid more wood on the fire.

The weather updates on the radio had gone from bad to worse, with reports of flooding and damage on the mainland coming more often. The wind was growing and the rain was relentless. Luke knew the island couldn't be faring much better, but at least they were dry inside.

"I wonder if they found my boat?" she asked.

"If they have, that's good, but with this weather, I wonder if they'll even go after it."

"I hope they have it already. Do you think if I called 911 I could get through to the coast guard."

He motioned to the phone. "Give it a shot."

He watched her reach for the receiver, put in a call and listened while she got transferred to the coast guard. After she'd explained who she was, she listened and he knew the news wasn't good. "Okay. I'll try to call tomorrow." She slowly set the receiver back in the cradle, and closed her eyes and shook her head.

"What did they say?" he asked.

She opened her eyes and slowly lifted them to him. She looked totally stressed. "They haven't found the boat yet. Too many emergencies with the storms. The good news is the GPS signal is still on and strong." She glanced out at the windows and cringed when a particularly strong gust of wind drove against the house. "I just wonder if when they do find it, it'll be in pieces. Maybe they won't find it at all."

He started to say that a boat probably would fair

better out in the open water than being battered against a dock, but didn't get a chance. Another gust of wind hurled against the house and a popping sound vibrated through the air.

He looked above them as if he could see through the ceiling and find the source of the explosive noise. Then it happened again, the crash muffled by the roar of the wind. He didn't wait to hear it again.

He jogged across the room, heading toward the side entrance.

"Where are you going?" Shay called.

"Out!"

She started running after him. "What's going on?" she asked when she caught up to him in the utility room as he stepped into his boots. He grabbed his poncho, slipped it over his head, then looked at her. He had an idea, and if he was right, they could be in a lot of trouble. "Just stay put and I'll be back."

Chapter Six

"You can't go out there," Shay protested, but it was as if she hadn't said a thing. Luke opened the door and a huge gust of cold and wetness rolled into the room before he stepped out without a look in her direction. As the door closed with a crack, she felt a surge of panic at being left alone. She heard another crash, and it was as if the whole house shook.

She hurried over to the door, but knew she couldn't go out there—she had no shoes and her jacket was back in the great room. Taking a deep breath, Shay reassured herself that Luke would be back. It was nothing. Just noises from the storm. She went back into the great room, sank down on the couch and had barely settled when she heard the door open.

"Come on! Shay, come on!" Luke yelled.

He ran into the room. "We have to get out of here!"

"What are you—?"

The look on his face stopped her dead. "Now," he

said, and grabbed at her, catching her arm and jerking her up off the couch.

"My jacket!" she gasped, twisting to reach for it.

She had it in her hands as Luke all but dragged her to the kitchen and headed toward the door. She twisted away from Luke when she saw a strike of lightning light up the heavens.

"We can't go out there," she said, but Luke tugged her jacket out of her hands.

"Get it on." She barely had time to put her arms in before he was pulling her toward the door again. Shay stumbled, but he held her, righting her, and kept going across the terrace onto the lawn and into the deluge. She couldn't lift her head into the stinging rain, and as Luke pulled her farther from the house, she kept her eyes on her feet. She stumbled again over a rock in the grass, stinging her bare foot.

Luke let her go and the wind was so strong she thought she might flip, then she felt his hand at her back, pushing her so hard she almost was off her feet sailing forward. She was out of control, then a sudden rushing sound filled the air, and she felt the sting of rain on her skin right before she hit the ground face first.

She tasted dirt and grass in her mouth. Her hands kneaded the soggy soil, and she pushed, half sinking into the ground as she struggled to her feet. Stunned for a moment, she was able to get air in her lungs and regain her balance.

She turned, unable to figure out what had

happened until she saw the house. The massive pines that had framed the south side were no longer standing. They'd been torn out of the ground by the wind and crashed onto the house. Branches embraced the structure, crushing it under their weight.

Terrified, she spun around, looking right and left for Luke, squinting into the rain as her heart rose in her throat. Then through the darkness, she saw movement off to the left. She put a hand up to shield her eyes and saw Luke. He lay half under the branches of a monstrous pine that had obliterated part of the house. He'd pushed her out of the way, then been hit as the trees had fallen.

She ran to him, capturing his hands, tugging with all her might to get him free. "Oh, God," she gasped. "Are you all right?"

He came tumbling toward her, sending them both back onto the soaking ground, him on top of her. She looked up into his dark face that was streaked with mud and dirt.

He gasped for air, then rolled to the right, away from her, onto his hands and knees. As she got to her feet, he did the same thing. He staggered at first, then steadied himself. The poncho was torn at the shoulder and caked with mud and pine needles.

He shook his head sharply as if to clear it, then stared at her, and she knew she wasn't in much better shape than he was at the moment.

"Luke?" she gasped, wanting to grab him, to feel his support, but stopped herself. "Are you hurt?"

He swiped at his clothes. "I'm in one piece," he muttered. "Damn trees."

She glanced back at the destruction that had taken a mere moment to happen, but could have killed them both. She covered her mouth with both hands, absorbing the horror. Oblivious to the pelting rain, she looked at Luke. "My God, we could have been killed."

His eyes were on the ruined house as rain ran down his face, flattening his hair to his scalp. "We weren't," he said in a flat tone, then turned away from the painful sight. "Let's get out of this."

She stared at the huge house that had been almost destroyed. "There's no place to go," she breathed, starting to shake from cold and shock.

Luke turned. "The guest house."

She glanced behind them at the small house in the distance. It was still intact. Luke headed toward it, and she hurried after him through the storm, which seemed to be growing in strength by the moment. He led the way around the side of the building and she followed him onto a deck and to a set of French doors. They weren't locked and opened when he pushed the latch.

They stepped into darkness, but it felt so safe and so wonderful. And the floor underfoot was smooth, something her feet greatly appreciated.

Luke closed the door. "Let me get the lights." She heard a clicking sound, then more as Luke flicked the switch a few more times. "The electricity's out," he said from the shadows.

Shay could make out a few shapes in the room,

maybe a couch and a chair, but not much more. She turned and saw a glow. She wasn't sure what was making it until she walked toward it and saw that Luke had turned on the gas burners of a stove. The light was low but enough to see the kitchen, a tiny space with limited counters and a refrigerator off to one side.

"There's gas—thank God—but I need to check and make sure there aren't any leaks from the main."

The scent of lemon oil that hung in the air of the main house was out here, too, but she couldn't smell gas. Luke walked around her, and said, "I'll be right back." With that he went back outside, and she could hear him on the deck, then nothing. Moments later, footsteps hit the wood and the door opened.

"Nothing I can find at the connections," he said, pushing his hood back and shaking his head before he glanced around. "We need more light than what the stove's offering. Stay right here. I think there's a lamp in the bedroom." She heard a door click open, then his feet as he shuffled around the room. Soon, another glow started to form in his direction.

Luke came back carrying an old-fashioned oil lamp. Finally, she could see her surroundings and they were about as she'd thought when she'd arrived. Furnishings were sparse—it had a couch, a table, a chair. No TV, radio or books were in sight. It looked as if the guest house had never been lived in.

She turned to Luke as he put the lamp down on the side table and let the mangled poncho slip off his shoulders and fall to the floor. At the same time the wind rattled the windows and rain hit the house, each drop sounding like a bullet.

She suddenly started to shiver, and it didn't have a lot to do with the cold and dampness all around her. She swallowed hard, the last glimpse she'd had of the main house coming to her in a rush. The huge structure had been destroyed, and they'd been in it moments before the devastation hit. "Oh, God," she whispered. "Thank you."

She didn't miss the quizzical expression that her thanks brought to his face. "What are you—?"

She let herself touch him on the arm and felt the heat of his skin under her fingertips. "You saved my life. You're a real hero."

His face twisted with what looked like pain to her. His reaction didn't make sense. "We got out," he said matter of factly and drew back from her touch. "And I'm no hero."

"Oh, yes," she breathed, but couldn't get out any more words to tell him how wrong he was. She started to shake, and tried to hug herself to stop it, but it didn't work. "W-we could have died," she choked out.

Luke was watching her from the shadows, then he did something that totally stunned her. He came closer and put his hands on her shoulders. He whispered, "It's okay. We got out." And she started to sob.

LUKE FELT AS AWKWARD as a teenager. He had Shay by her shoulders, and all he really wanted to do was pull her to him and make things better. But he couldn't. All he could do was stand there, feeling her tremble. Then she pressed a hand to his chest, placing it over his heart, and almost fell against him.

He slowly let himself put his arms around her, closing his eyes tightly, and he held her. Her cries shook her body, and he felt a pain in him that he'd never known before. He couldn't do a thing to help her. He wished he could, he would have if he could have. But he didn't know what to do, so he just held her until her sobs started to ease, and he heard her sniffling as she slowly moved back.

She swiped at her eyes, and in the low glow from the lamp, he saw her smear mud across her face. "I—I really am okay," she breathed. "I'm not a crier. I really am not a crier. I don't know why I did that."

"Shock," he said.

She looked up, the light playing shadows at her eyes and throat. "Yes, shock," she agreed.

She turned from him and seemed to be studying the space around them. At least she didn't bring up his being a hero again.

"Any chance this place has heat?" Even he had to agree that the air was far too cold for any degree of comfort. "Does it have a furnace?"

He didn't know. "I can check on it," he said.

She motioned to the stone fireplace. "Maybe we can find some wood?"

"Maybe," he said, not about to promise to go looking for firewood in this weather right then.

She looked down at the water and mud puddling at her feet. "Bare feet again," she said, and laughed softly. He was afraid it would turn to hysteria, but didn't. "Wet and dirty, but alive," she continued in a low voice.

He walked around her into the kitchen and shut off the burners. He really was worried about a gas leak, particularly at the main house, and there was no point in taking any chances until he could check it out.

"Luke, is there a phone out here?"

"There's one on the table in there."

"Well, this is definitely an emergency, so I'll call 911." He heard her pick up the phone. "Oh, shoot."

"What?" he asked.

"It's dead." She turned. "The trees must have damaged the phone lines, too." She picked up the lamp and walked past him into the kitchen. He watched her open the refrigerator door, look inside, then step back. "There's water and some food in there."

"The staff that cleans and stocks the house work down here, too. They've stayed here when the ferry goes down because of weather or whatever. There should be enough supplies for an emergency."

She opened and closed the cupboards one by one, then turned to him. The mud was still on her face and now it was streaked from her tears. "I guess even if we find a radio, it wouldn't be of any use." She pulled open a drawer. "Oh, yeah," she said, and held up a box of votive candles. "Let there be light."

Glancing around she carried the box over to the

hearth and put the lamp down. She opened the box and set the candles out in a row. She held out a hand to Luke. "Lighter or matches?" she asked.

"What?"

"You lit the oil lamp. What did you use?"

He fished a box of wooden matches out of his jeans pocket and handed them to her. She lit one candle after the other, and the light began to dispel the shadows in the room.

"Nice, while they last," he said as she straightened after lighting the last one.

"Right now it's great," she said.

The windows in the room rattled, and she flashed a look at them. "What about the trees around this place? Couldn't they fall over, too?"

"We'll find out," he said, going over to the door.

He knew that wasn't what she wanted to hear, but she didn't ask again. Instead, she picked up the lamp and approached him. "I hope for your boss's sake that he's got good insurance, and that more trees don't collapse on the house."

Luke shrugged. "They're just things."

"Easy for you to say," she murmured. "But I'd bet your boss wouldn't be so blasé about it."

"Maybe not," he agreed. "but what can you do? Things happen. Life goes on."

She shivered, no doubt from her wet clothes.

She headed into the kitchen, and turned on the faucet. After a minute or so, she could feel the water heat up.

"Thank goodness! I'm sure we could both use a hot shower," she said.

He wouldn't argue with that. His shoulder throbbed, and he could feel grit and dampness in his boots. "A shower sounds good, but getting back into dirty, wet clothes isn't very appealing."

"Maybe there are some clothes around here we could use? You said the cleaning crews stayed a few times, and who knows what they could have left behind?"

"There haven't been any guests in a long time, and the staff…who knows?" he said.

"I'll look around," she said, and picked up the lamp to take it with her.

Luke stayed where he was, watching the night and the storm. He heard her poking around in the other room, then had an idea. There was a closet by the front door, and he remembered the cleaning staff kept a stockpile of supplies for the main house in there. It was worth a look to see what was there.

He'd barely opened it when Shay called out, "Luke?"

Her voice came through the darkness, and he wondered why just the sound of it ran riot over his nerves. Her voice was like liquid gold, smooth and fluid and rich.

"In here, by the front door. Bring the lamp with you." The glow from the candles barely touched the inside of the closet, and he couldn't make out anything except dark shadows.

Shay came up to him, lamp in her hand. A near
drowning and a life-and-death run would have left
most women bedraggled and miserable-looking,
but not Shay. Her damp curls and clinging shirt—
even the smear of mud on her face—just made her
look more... He brushed away the thought, unwill-
ing to go there.

He took the lamp from her, then held it up to see
inside the closet. Shelves of cleaning supplies, along
with mops and brooms, lined the space. One shelf
held nothing but folded towels. He felt as if he'd
struck gold. He reached and picked up a couple of
T-shirts.

"Here, hold this," he said to Shay, handing her the
lamp. Then he shook out the top shirt.

"Nice," she murmured, with more than a bit of
sarcasm and he looked down at the shirt. *I Luv
Pirates* was written across the front.

"A souvenir from the festival the islanders had a
while back. One of the cleaning crew probably kept
them here to change into," he suggested.

"You know, Bartholomew Grace built this place.
He's one of the most dreaded pirates that ever lived."

Yes, Luke did know, but he wondered how she did.
"How did you know?"

She reached for the other shirt and shook it out; it
was a duplicate of the first. "I was checking on something about the rights to the beaches around here for
my research, and it came up. The rumor was, at one
point, that he stayed here so his enemies would not

see him as vulnerable. I guess the rest of the time he was at that huge estate that the Graces still own."

"You're a historian, too?"

"Oh, no, just part of my research. Just because I'm a marine biologist doesn't mean the field doesn't touch areas connected with it, like Lost Point. It's so isolated, but if this area's like the rest of the beaches up on this end, marine life has been inexplicably dying."

Although she'd mentioned this earlier, now that he thought about it, he'd seen some dead fish on the beach, more than he had in the past. "So, you want to find the animals, test them, and…?"

"That's the point. I haven't been able to study the beaches up here. The owner just won't answer any calls or letters or anything. Not even a 'get lost' for me." He saw her frown up at him. "You've done so much for me, and I hate to ask for more, but is there any way you could get me in touch with the owner of Lost Point?"

They had just escaped with their lives—barely— and she was asking for favors? He might have laughed if he'd thought there was any humor in the situation. She'd almost died getting here, and all because she wanted to find out what was killing the marine life. It didn't seem like a fair trade to him— her for the denizens of the deep.

"Next time I talk to him, I'll tell him."

"Thanks so much," she said.

"Sure." Grabbing some towels, he shut the closet and turned. He heard her following him, and saw the glow from the lamp, and he stopped by the couch.

"I wish the storm would just go away," she said, putting the lamp back on the side table. "But, I guess if I were really wishing, I'd make it count and ask for it to be summertime. How about you?"

He watched the way the light from the lamp flickered on her face and wondered when his ability to wish had died. He remembered wishing after he'd come home that his experience in Iraq had all been an illusion, that life was the same as it had been before he'd left, that his buddy Chance would come up to him, give him a hug and laugh about their adventures. But those wishes were doomed from the start. Chance was gone forever. He hadn't come back with Luke. The life Luke had known was gone, too. Now he didn't wish at all—there was no point.

"No wishes," he said.

She stood there watching him.

"What?" he asked.

"Nothing." She shook her head and would have turned if he hadn't pressed the point.

"Just say what you want to say."

She hesitated, then said, "Okay, you don't seem very upset with the house and the stuff in it. It has to be a total loss. Doesn't that bother you?"

He had nothing to lose anymore. "What should I do?" he asked. "It's a house. Things," he said."

"To you maybe, but what about your boss? Is he that indifferent to this place? To lose all of this is terrible."

Compared to what he'd already lost, this was

nothing. He turned his back to her and approached the doors. "Take a shower and clean up."

"Oh, my God," she gasped. The next thing he knew, she was touching his back.

He spun around at the contact, surprised by the sudden pain he felt. Shay stood there, the T-shirt she'd been holding on the floor. She held the lamp in one hand, and lifted her other one. In the dim light he could see something dark on her fingers. Blood. *His* blood. He reached over and touched his back, a burning sensation exploding across his left shoulder blade as he did.

"Oh, God, you're hurt," she whispered. "You're bleeding."

Chapter Seven

Shay was almost thankful for the lack of light, afraid to see the damage done to Luke's back. A tree limb must have punctured the poncho and cut deeply through the shirt into his skin, but he hadn't noticed. Maybe it was shock or simple adrenaline. She stared at her fingers, at the blood, then at Luke.

"It's nothing," he said.

But it was. She knew and he knew it.

"I'll try to find a first-aid kit, or some clean cloths and disinfectant or something," she said in a rush.

"No," Luke countered almost immediately. He trailed his fingers over his shoulder until she knew he felt the wound. He grimaced for just a moment, then dropped his hand to his side. "I'll take care of it."

"I hope there's some first-aid supplies around here somewhere."

"I'll take care of it," he said again more firmly, and it shut her up.

She hated the sticky feel of the blood on her

fingers and rubbed them on her damp jeans. "Okay," she finally said softly.

His eyes flicked over her and the wound on his back seemed to be forgotten. "Go and shower. Get out of those cold clothes."

"No, you first," she said quickly.

"I'll take care of myself. There's a bathroom off the bedroom. Take the light with you."

"You'll be in the dark," she said with what she thought was simple logic.

"The candles are still burning, and I'm not going anywhere, so I don't have to see around the place. Take your shower."

With no other option given to her, Shay took the lamp, crouched to pick up the T-shirt, then headed off. She was tempted by the old-fashioned claw-foot tub in the bathroom, but stepped into the small shower stall and turned on the water. She rushed through it, only taking extra time when the water first ran warm over her chilled skin. She hurried to finish and dress, putting on the silly T-shirt.

She pushed her hair back behind her ears, then went out into the main room. Luke was sitting on the floor with his back to her, his head pressed to his knees. He hadn't changed, but she could see a bit of white material showing through the tear in his bloodied shirt.

He looked up, even though she was certain she hadn't made any noise in her bare feet, and shifted, pushing up to stand. "Hot water?" he asked.

"Plenty, thanks," she said. "How's your back?"

"It's okay," he said dismissively.

"You found some bandages?"

He rolled his head as if to loosen up the muscles in his shoulders and back. When he flinched, she knew his wound wasn't "nothing." "I found some gauze and tape in a kitchen drawer."

She started to ask about disinfectant, but thought better of it. Instead, she said, "It's your turn to put on your stupid T-shirt."

He glanced at hers, then at her face. "Stupid? It looks pretty damn good."

"Sure," she murmured. "Don't you think someone who would own a shirt like this would be, maybe, sixteen years old and have an MP3 player always plugged into her ears?"

He cocked his head to one side, those dark eyes intent on her. "Or be a middle-aged man who found a shirt cheap and bought it, and about all he'd have plugged into his ear would be a hearing aid."

Now, was that a joke? She studied him for a moment, then decided it wasn't even close. "I'm rooting for the teenager," she said as she took the lamp and went over to the closet by the front door. "And who knows what else might be in here?"

"What are you doing?" he asked.

"Looking for a radio and not a hearing aid."

"I'm going to go back out to look around again and double-check on the gas line," he said.

She stopped. "Is that safe?"

"Sure. I won't get near enough for trouble. I just want to take a look near the main house." He grabbed the torn poncho, then stepped into his boots. With a glance back at her, he slipped on the poncho and opened the door. Then he was gone.

She went over to the closet and pulled the door open, holding the lamp high to see inside. She scanned the cleaning supplies, saw the shelf where Luke had pulled the shirts out from under folded towels, and buckets stacked in one corner. She stepped back, reaching for the door knob when the light flashed to something on a shelf just above eye level.

She stood on her tiptoes to get a better look, then saw a metal scraper, but right beside it was what looked like a portable radio. Pulling it off the shelf, she looked down at the radio with no cord dangling out of it.

"Bingo!"

Putting the lamp on the side table, she turned the radio over and saw a battery compartment. She slipped it open, saw six batteries all in a row, then closed it up. Literally holding her breath, she pushed the power switch. When a green light flashed by the knob, she exhaled in a rush.

She fiddled with the dial, heard static, then music. The oldies song sounded wonderful to her.

The door suddenly opened startling her, and Luke almost staggered into the room. He pushed the door shut, then turned and tugged at the poncho, letting it slip to the floor.

"Good news and bad news. The good news is, there's no gas leak. And I looked for a bypass on the electric service panel."

"Was there?"

He ran both hands over his face, then skimmed them back and over his hair. "No. The main line was torn out when the trees went over, so no electricity. And worse news?"

She grimaced. "That's not the bad news?"

"It's bad, just not really bad."

"What's really bad?"

"The heat in here is electric and the temperature has dropped a lot. I've never seen it get so cold, so fast. The rain feels like ice out there now."

She realized then that chilliness that hung in the air was starting to feel frigid. "There's blankets in the bedroom on the bed—I saw them stacked there. And if we can find something to use for firewood, we can have a bit of heat, at least in here."

He glanced down at her hands. "What's that?"

She'd almost forgotten. She held up the radio and the song "The Twist" bounced around the room. "Look what I found in the closet. The batteries are good, so we can get the news and weather."

"Right in between doing the twist and saying hello to Mary Lou?" he asked.

This time she knew he was making a joke. She went closer to him, tipping her face up to study his, and she was sure some of the tension eased from his expression. "I don't believe it," she said.

He looked perplexed now. "What, that the electricity's out completely?"

"Oh, no, that I believe; but what I don't believe is that you just sort of made a joke. Okay, it wasn't a laugh-out-loud kind of joke, but it was a mildly amusing one."

"What joke?"

She shrugged. "If you have to explain it, it loses its punch."

He stared down at her, hard, then suddenly she saw something she hadn't seen on the man ever. His lips actually twitched upward for a moment, and the change in his face was remarkable. Years dropped from him. "You think that was funny?"

She couldn't believe that something so tiny as his response felt like such a victory for her. "Actually, I do."

"You're easily amused," he murmured, and she held her breath, waiting for the real smile to come.

"I guess so," she said when the smile never materialized. "But we've got music, and sooner or later, weather and news. Food's in the kitchen, and if we can find firewood, we might get warm, too."

"Sounds like a plan to me," Luke said, and despite his stony expression, Shay knew that the softening she saw in the man, however slight it was, had been real.

"Good, then it's your turn to have a shower, and meanwhile, I'll see what I can do to get us settled for the night."

He didn't move. "What were you in a past life, a teacher or a drill sergeant?"

Another near joke? Maybe there was hope for him yet. "No, just bossy in this life," she said.

He raised one eyebrow. "I'd say so," he responded.

She held the lamp out to him. "You'll need this."

He shook his head. "No, I'm fine," he said, then headed into the bedroom. The door shut behind him, and moments later, she heard the water start. A smile from Luke? Oddly, that seemed like something to strive for, she thought as she went into the kitchen.

She stood in there, the light from the lamp revealing there was nothing much of use. Not even a table and chairs that they could break up to burn. There was the small refrigerator, a few cupboards, the stove, a counter, and that was it.

She made her way back to the hearth, where the candles were burning down, and she knew that, in a short while, they'd go out. So much for the extra light.

She sat down on the raised brick, and felt something scrape against her calf. She looked down, but couldn't make out what it was. With the help of one of the candles, she could see what looked like a handle of some sort. She pulled on it, and a box slid out from under the hearth. In the dim candlelight, she saw a full wood box.

"Eureka," she breathed, and pulled out some logs to stack in the empty hearth. She'd made a lot of fires when she and Graham had been on assignment in less than luxurious accommodations, and with the matches, she soon had the fire started.

The wood snapped and flared, and soon it caught and heat slowly started to invade the chill in the room. Pleased with herself, she turned, and almost ran into Luke, who had just come out of the bedroom.

His damp hair was slicked back from his face, and the fire caught gold highlights in it that she hadn't noticed before. The same glow caught the paleness of the scar that cut through his eyebrow. He had on the fresh shirt, with his own Levi's. His feet were bare. The shirt was tighter on him than it was on her, and the material was tested by the width of his shoulders. He glanced past her at the fire, watching the flames leap and crackle as if mesmerized by them.

"Luke?" She could see the fire flicker in his dark eyes. "Luke?" she said again, and reached to touch his arm.

He'd reacted so violently to her touch in the truck that she was stunned that he didn't respond when she laid her fingers on his cool, bare arm. She could almost feel his pulse under her touch. "Luke?"

LUKE SAW FIRE everywhere, the heat intense on his skin, scorching him, but he couldn't move. Then he felt something, a connection, a lifeline that had never been there before. But before he could figure out what it was, he saw Shay standing in front of him, watching him with concern. Startled by the emotions her touch evoked in him, he pulled away from it and the fire; swallowing hard, he realized it wasn't the touch he wanted to disappear, it was the heat.

He walked slowly toward the rear doors, barely aware of the way the rain had changed to beads of hail that rattled the glass and were collecting on the deck.

A connection? He shivered and touched the glass. Cold seeped through his skin, and he welcomed it, the way it could shut out the flames and the heat and give him a reprieve from...

He closed his eyes as he shook his head sharply. A reprieve. Then a thought came out of nowhere. From being alone? So alone. Always alone.

"Luke?"

Shay's voice was soft and gentle, and he closed his eyes more tightly, but nothing could shut out the way his name sounded when she said it.

"Luke," she repeated, closer now, directly behind him. He heard her take a breath before saying, "Are you okay?"

Had he ever been okay? Maybe in a past life. A long time ago. He brushed a hand roughly over his face. "Sure," he lied. "Where did you get the wood?"

"There was a stocked fire box under the hearth. With luck, we'll have some heat for a while."

Heat. God, he hated the heat. He yearned for cold air so he could breathe. "Good," he lied again. "Great."

Hail beat on the glass, surprising Shay. "Oh, gosh," she said, coming to his side to look out at what he was seeing.

"What did the news say?" he asked, catching her reflection in the glass. He wasn't paying attention to the hail now, but her. Her large eyes were shadowed, and the way she tilted her head to one side studying the weather, made her hair drift around her shoulders.

"Oh, I didn't hear it yet. I turned it off while I did some exploring and made the fire. The batteries…" He saw her shrug, an oddly vulnerable action under the ugly T-shirt. "I have no idea how old they are, or how long they'll last, so I wanted to conserve them."

She moved away from him, taking a great deal of heat with her. He breathed a bit easier. She crossed to the radio where it sat on the hearth. Turning it on, she fiddled with the dial then glanced back at him. "This is odd. There's another thing on the top that looks like a dial, but different. Do you know what it's for?"

Of course he did; it was his radio. He'd just forgotten it was here at all. He actually didn't remember bringing it to the guest house when he came to Lost Point. His best guess was that Maurice had done it, but hadn't told him. Luke went over to her and hunkered down by the radio. "It's a weather band."

"Terrific," she said, and he was quite sure if he'd looked at her right then, she would have been bouncing with excitement. He wasn't as thrilled. The damn thing had never worked in the past, but he gave it a shot. He aligned the tuner, made sure it was dead-on the signal stripe, but it didn't pick up any weather band. He sank back on his heels and glanced up at Shay.

She frowned down at him. "I guess we'll have to depend on the oldies station."

He flipped it to AM, turned the tuner and the next

thing, music came out. He straightened and moved back, away from the radiating heat of the fire. "I wouldn't keep it near the hearth if you don't want it to melt," he said.

Shay reached for the radio and took it to the couch, where she put it on the side table. The music continued, and Luke was actually glad to have it going since it meant he didn't have to have a conversation with her. Then the news came on.

He watched Shay sink down on the couch as they both listened to the report. He didn't miss the way her hands clenched as she stared at the radio. The storm was shifting, the stream colder now, and despite the winds not letting up, the temperature was dropping rapidly. Parts of the mainland were without electricity, and fears for people trapped in their houses without heat were growing. To Luke, it sounded like a war zone, and he shivered. He knew that they were well and truly on their own for the duration.

The newscaster continued, but Luke was no longer listening; he knew enough. The hail on the windows only underscored their situation. Then the news ended, and the announcer introduced the next song. "Three hours to go before the new year," he said with enthusiasm that sounded forced at best.

"This is horrible," Shay finally said as she pulled her legs up to sit cross-legged on the couch. "But I guess we have it better than a lot of others do."

Yes, they did. He realized he was better off because Shay was here. Luke was actually thankful that she'd washed up on his beach and that she had had to stay. She let him focus on what had to be done, what he needed to do to make sure she would be okay rather than worrying about his own demons.

"We've got blankets. And with the fire going, we can bank it and keep the chill off during the night," he said.

"Luke, I'm glad you're here with me," she said out of the blue, almost echoing his own thoughts about her as if she'd read his mind.

Words stuck in his throat. A simple "Me, too," would have been the right thing to say—and the truth. But he couldn't get it out. Instead, he nodded and said, "You know, I can probably get back into the main house in the morning and get some things we might need out here. Some clothes, maybe food."

She blinked at him. "You can't go back in there."

"I'll take a quick look when it gets light. If I can, I will. I'll get whatever I can find. There's no telling how long this is going to last. And the more wood we have, the better."

"If you find some fresh clothes, does that mean I have to give up this T-shirt?"

"That's a joke, right?" he asked.

"Absolutely."

"I thought so." He was learning.

She nodded as if with approval, then glanced at the fire before meeting his gaze again. "I've been thinking. We should both sleep out here. There's probably not enough wood to heat the bedrooms, so it's best to stay nearby. We can get the mattress off the bed, and one of us can use it and the other one can sleep on the couch."

He had no plans to sleep around her, but he wasn't going to argue about it, either. "We'll work it out," was all he said. "But we do need to check on the available blankets and extra pillows." He headed for the bedroom.

"You don't have to do that right now."

Yes, he did. He really did. He found three blankets on the bed and in a small closet he found three more, plus a thick comforter and four pillows. He left most of them on the bed, but took two blankets and a pillow into the living area. Shay sat on the couch, and she looked up when he came back. "What are you doing?"

"I found quite a few linens, and I left them on the bed for you. They should keep you warm enough. I'll sleep on the couch."

"No, I will," she said, sitting up straighter.

He looked down at her. "No, you won't. You'll be in the bedroom, and you'll keep the door shut, just as you promised to do before we had to move out here. You'll stay in there no matter what and we'll get through this."

She sank back into the cushions and grudgingly nodded. "Okay. But only if you'll really sleep on the couch, not by the doors on the floor."

God, that look was back—that "poor guy" look—and he hated it. "I'm used to sleeping on the floor. By the doors is as good as anyplace for me."

She glanced out the window, then back at him. "Why?"

"I told you, I'm claustrophobic and—"

"No, it's not that, is it? It's not claustrophobia."

He wanted to argue, and he tried to, but anything he thought to say seemed wrong to him. He finally dropped down on the other end of the couch and admitted something to her that he hadn't told anyone before. "It's crazy, but I feel closed in, and the walls, they keep me from…" He tried to stop the words, but it was too late. "They keep me from being free." He closed his eyes tightly. "It's the walls."

He turned from Shay, from her watchful eyes, which stared at him as if he were some sort of caged animal. It took all the control he had not to bolt for the door. He took a breath before facing the woman he'd known such a short time, but who seemed to be able to see more of him than anyone had in a very long time. "It's the walls," he said again in a low voice.

The pity in her expression was fading, and she said softly, "I know about walls. After Graham died, I couldn't stay in a room alone. I couldn't explain it, but I just couldn't do it. I felt trapped or closed in." She clasped her hands in front of her tightly. "No one understood. But it was the walls, the four walls. And I felt empty."

God, his stomach hurt. He thought it was from her defining his own pain, but he knew that wasn't it, not entirely. He hurt for her. For what he could only guess she'd gone through in losing her husband. And it was for a man who had been so loved by her that life had been almost impossible for her when he was gone.

"And now?" Luke whispered over the raging sounds of the storm outside.

"I don't know when it happened, but I looked up one day after working in my office at home, and it was okay. The room was just a room. The walls were just walls, and I could walk out if I wanted to, or stay if I wanted to."

"Just like that?"

She gave him a small smile. "Not really. It actually took me almost a year to get to that point, and I was in therapy for a while."

He found himself wondering something. "Your husband—you were married a long time?"

Grief flashed across her face, then it was gone. "No, not even a year. Just seven months. Not long enough. Not long enough at all. Our two-year anniversary was—or would have been—yesterday. But we never got to celebrate even one."

Luke had thought that the short time had to have been incredible between them if she could love Graham that deeply. But he didn't want to know. He didn't want to hear about her and Graham anymore.

"I'll sleep on the couch," he finally said.

"Luke?" She touched her lips with her tongue, and he could sense her hesitation. "You were in the service, weren't you?"

He flinched at the question, but tried to cover it. "Why are you asking?"

"I just thought…you mentioned your problems, and I thought maybe that's where you had your trouble."

What was she? Clairvoyant? "How did you know about me being…there?"

She blushed, she actually blushed. Color rose in her cheeks and her eyes dropped to her hands. "I'm sorry, but I was looking for a robe in the closet last night and I saw a jacket in there. It looked like an officer's jacket or something. I figured it must be yours." She finally lifted her gaze to his. "I really do apologize for snooping like that. I didn't mean to intrude."

He didn't give a damn about her being in his closet, or her seeing the jacket. What he cared about was her being able to figure him out so easily, and if she knew who he really was, would she give a damn? "Why do you figure that if I'm screwed up, it comes from that?"

"The therapy group I was in…? There was a man named Roy in it. Just first names, you know. Nothing more. He had problems and they came from his time in the army in Desert Storm. There were things he couldn't talk about that made his life pretty hard for him to get through."

Luke's hands were clenched so hard that his nails dug into his palms. "So, you assumed that I'm like this Roy?" he asked, hearing the tightness growing in his voice.

"No, no," she said quickly. "I just thought that with you being alone, and the claustrophobia, and the walls that maybe…" She shrugged, a fluttery movement of her shoulders under the clinging T-shirt. "I'm sorry. I shouldn't have said anything."

"What did this Roy have? Post-traumatic stress disorder, or some other alphabet-soup named problem? Or was he just plain crazy?"

She flinched at his words, and he wished he didn't care, but he hated all of this.

"No, he wasn't crazy," she said quietly. "No, he wasn't. He just was sick."

Just sick. "Sure," he murmured, and he got up and went to the doors. He stared out at the hail that was building at the base of the frame.

"You know, I'll go and see if there's some coffee in the kitchen. It'll help us warm up." She got the lamp, then hurried out of the room.

He didn't say a thing, just stared at his own reflection in the frosted glass in front of him. He waited until she was in the kitchen before he gave in to the need to open the door. He felt the stinging brush of hail on his face, took a deep breath, then closed the door again.

"Just sick," he whispered. Add being a traitor to that and you had Lucas Roman. Lucas Roman. The sick traitor.

He heard her bustling about, and he actually found himself wishing that when Shay Donovan left the island after this was all over, she'd never find out whom she'd been with. He wished that she'd never hear the name Lucas Roman or ever find out what he did.

Chapter Eight

Shay was shaking and had to put the lamp down on the counter before she dropped it. She pressed both hands to the cold tiles for a long moment while she made herself calm down. She didn't know why she'd told Luke anything more about Graham, or more important, about herself. Or why she'd tried to get Luke to talk about his problems. But the look on his face when he'd made the comments about the walls had torn at her, and she'd wanted to help him take the edge off. Instead, she'd exposed some of herself to him, and it had made her feel painfully vulnerable.

The man was little more than a stranger. The fact was, she didn't even know his last name. But he'd saved her life. She owed him more than she could say, and obviously he never planned to let her pay off her debt. There was something about him that made her want to reach out, to help him ease the weight on his shoulders, to make him smile. That made her almost laugh, but it never came. She pushed back from the counter and resumed her search for the coffee.

She found a jar of instant coffee and a small pot to heat the water on the stove. As the water boiled, she spooned the coffee into two mugs, filling them when the water was ready. Walking into the living room, she saw Luke laying another log on the fire. Putting the coffee down on the end table, she turned on the radio to catch the news.

"I can find some crackers or something to nibble on, if you'd like," she said to Luke.

He shook his head, then glanced at the coffee. "Just the coffee."

She lifted one mug and held it out to him. He took it between both hands. "Thanks," he murmured.

"I wish we'd brought some wine with us," she said as she sank down onto the couch.

He slanted her a look after taking a drink of his coffee. "Next time we don't have to run for our lives, we'll grab a few bottles."

Now that was a joke, and she grinned at him. "That was pretty good."

"I'm working on it." He moved to the doors as if honing in on the only spot in the room where he felt a degree of comfort and ease. "I think the hail's letting up. It's too dark to tell, but at least it's not hitting the windows anymore."

"Good," she breathed and sipped her own coffee as Luke went to the kitchen.

Finally the music stopped and the DJ gave a

weather update. "Two hours to midnight. One hundred and twenty minutes of the old year left before it's gone. Then it's a new year and a new beginning."

A new beginning? Despite her odd circumstances, she as inclined to agree with the announcer. She was totally removed from her old life and was living a new one that she'd never known existed before. No familiar people or places, just Luke, the island and the storm.

She jumped when she saw that Luke had stealthily come up beside her. Looking up at him, she could hear her heart racing from the man's closeness. "Okay, we need to make a deal," she said.

"What kind of deal?" he asked.

"Please, you promised that you'd let me know when you were sneaking up on me." She pressed a hand to her heart. "I thought you were still in the kitchen."

"If I was sneaking, why would I warn you?" he asked.

She cocked her head to one side and studied him. "When you're right, you're right," she chuckled, and watched with great satisfaction as his lips began to twitch. "*And* you're almost smiling."

He shrugged. "You make it sound as if I just walked on water."

It wasn't that close to a miracle, but that didn't stop her breath from catching when his shadowy smile lingered longer. "It's just nice," she said honestly.

Luke looked away, and she thought for a moment that she'd embarrassed him. He glanced back at her as she watched him and lifted one eyebrow. "Is there something I should know about the coffee?"

"Excuse me?"

"You're the one acting so serious, you make me wonder if I should be worried that there's something in the coffee."

She met his dark gaze. "Yet another attempt at a joke?"

"Could be," he replied, and the hint of a grin on his lips was very intriguing.

"The coffee's fine, or at least as fine as instant coffee can ever be," she said, heading back into the kitchen to make herself another cup.

When she returned, Luke was on the couch, so she took the opposite end. The two of them sat silently, sipped coffee and watched the fire. They left the radio on and music mingled with the pop and crackle of the burning wood. The conversation was skimpy, but Shay felt comfortable and snug in the small house with Luke.

He drained his coffee, then rested the mug on his thigh. "It's been a while since I've seen weather like this."

"In Seattle or elsewhere?" she asked as she fingered her cup.

He shook his head. "Years ago I lived on the east coast, up in northern New York State. Storms there could be real killers."

That was probably the most personal information he'd offered without her prodding. "I was in Maine for the winter once, and it was so cold, my face ached when I was outside. I never went back," she said.

"You had family there?" he asked.

"No. Graham was there for a seminar, and I went along." They'd been married less than a month and there had been no way she would have stayed behind in San Diego. "We thought it would be like a delayed honeymoon." She found she could actually smile at that memory now, that it didn't make her ache the way it had after Graham died and she could talk about it without choking up.

"We ended up going to Barbados right after we got home, to warm up and have the elusive honeymoon."

"Are you one of those people who always sees the glass as half-full?" he asked.

"Oh, no. I tend to get pretty worked up over things, Graham always saw the upside in anything. If the car blew up, he'd say that at least we didn't have to feel guilty buying a new car."

"Your car blew up?"

She caught at the memory of her and Graham's old van sitting on the side of the road in southern Mexico, with steam coming out of the engine, and from below, too. "No, not actually. It just sort of seized up when it overheated, then it started making this knocking sound. So Graham got a new van without a twinge of guilt."

"A true optimist," he murmured.

She nodded, and that was when her throat tightened on her, but it didn't the way it had been. She felt sad that Graham was gone, but that wrenching pain that had torn at her with every thought of him since he died wasn't there. She had the strangest feeling that she'd passed some milestone.

"Graham grew up poor, and he overcame so much, I guess things like a car breaking down weren't that big a deal to him. He just kept going and made the best of things."

"A really great guy," he acknowledged.

She found herself wanting to tell Luke just how wonderful Graham had been, but she bit her lip to stop the words. She stored them away for herself.

When she met Luke's gaze, its intensity shook her. She tried to think of something to say, something neutral. "So, how long did you live out east?"

"Until…" He stopped, then finished with, "Until I left home."

"For college?"

"At first," he said, then drained his coffee and stood. He crossed to the hearth and put another log on the fire. When it caught, he headed for the kitchen.

She heard the rattle of dishes and called, "I can make you more coffee."

"No problem," he said.

She shrugged and reached to turn the radio off. But she hesitated when the announcer said, "Thirty minutes to midnight, then it's goodbye to this year and hello to the next. Now from the national weather service…"

"Same old, same old," Luke said as the weather report ended.

Shay turned as he came out of the shadows. The candles had long since flickered out, and other than the oil lamp, the fire was the only light remaining.

"Yeah, I'm afraid so." She looked past him into the kitchen. "You should have taken the lamp with you."

He shrugged and crossed to the hearth, staring down at the fire. "The thing about darkness is, once you've seen where you're going, rooms don't change." He stood back. "Ten steps from the back door to the kitchen. Four feet from the refrigerator to the sink. Five steps from there to the stove. Six paces to the bathroom door from the bedroom door.

"In the main house, it's eleven steps from the utility room to the stove in the kitchen. Six more to the sinks." He spoke in a low tone, and she had the oddest feeling he wasn't talking to her now. "Seven steps from the wall to the door to get outside."

She'd heard of blind people getting around by counting steps, but he wasn't blind. "Why do you do that?"

"Being in the dark doesn't mean you can't see," he said in little more than a whisper.

She tucked her legs under her and pressed herself into the corner, never looking away from Luke. She didn't know why she felt as if his needing to "see" in the dark was life and death to him.

The radio blared, "Fifteen minutes to midnight. Get ready, Seattle. The new year is coming!"

Luke glanced at the radio, then at Shay, and un-expectedly answered her question. "When you don't have light at your command, you learn quickly to memorize your surroundings. If a light comes on, you burn the exposed images into your mind, then you have them forever. No one can get them away from you. Six steps to the door from the bed. The light was exactly eight feet above the floor. The keyhole, three feet from the floor."

She didn't understand any more than she had before he'd started the explanation. "When would you need to have that information?"

He sighed. "In another life. Long ago."

She leaned to pick up her coffee mug and finished the last of it. "It's almost midnight," she said to fill the silence.

He turned to look at her as the radio began the count down. "Five, four, three…"

Shay kept her eyes on Luke.

"…two, one! Happy New Year!" The strains of "Auld Lang Syne" mixed with laughter and cheering and horns being blown.

"Happy new year," Shay said to Luke.

He studied her, then said flatly, "Yeah, happy new year."

She watched him turn and crouch down in front of the fire. Then she saw something that wasn't a trick of the eye or a shadow. Putting her mug down, she moved over to Luke and swallowed hard as she looked at his back. A bloodstain was spreading across the shoulder of his T-shirt. "Luke, you're bleeding again."

LUKE TWISTED TO TOUCH his shoulder and saw the blood that darkened his fingertips. "Oh, dammit," he muttered. He'd thought he'd managed to staunch the blood with the gauze pad earlier. He'd been wrong.

"I'll be right back," Shay said, and went into the kitchen. He heard her open and close a couple of drawers before she came back. She'd found the gauze Luke had used earlier, and the roll of tape. But she'd also found a package of Band-Aids and some antibiotic spray. She put the things down on the table, then looked at him. "Come here and take off your shirt."

"I'll do it," he said and crossed to get the medical supplies himself, but Shay stood firmly between him and his target.

"You tried to fix it yourself already, and you're bleeding again. I'll do it this time." When he hesitated, she went on. "I'm actually certified for CPR and first-aid." She said that as if she'd just told him she was a doctor, then added, as if it sealed the deal, "Graham insisted on being certified in case of emergencies for those times when we weren't close to medical facilities."

He didn't care if Graham had trained her to be a damned neurosurgeon, he wasn't going to let her do anything to him. "I can handle it."

"You can't," she said bluntly. "Now just sit down on the chair and let me take a look at it."

His instinct to walk out on her came full force. That had been his way to deal with anything lately, and at any other time, with any other person, he would have done just that. But he knew she'd probably run after him out into the cold. He wouldn't get away. She was so damn stubborn about things. About the sleeping arrangement, about him staying at the house. So he grabbed the only chair, a straight-back with vinyl-covered seat, and turned it around to straddle it. He reached for the hem of his T-shirt, but Shay got to it first.

He flinched as he felt the dried blood catch on the cotton when she lifted his shirt, baring his back. He closed his eyes, held his breath, and the silly music surrounded him.

It had been a long time since he'd even looked at his back, but what he'd told her about images being burned in his mind, he remembered. He knew what she saw beyond the injury he'd gotten from the fallen tree. It wasn't a lot, just enough. A single scar at his waist. He'd thought it would eventually go away— and rope burns should have—but it lingered, pale against his skin. He'd done it to himself when he'd escaped, taking the pain to get the freedom.

He was a bit surprised that Shay didn't comment on it. He knew it wasn't the scar he cared about her seeing, it was the questions that would come, simple curiosity, but talking about it would bring back the horrible memories. And in the end, the truth was all that would be left.

He felt her fingers press against his skin, and he jumped involuntarily.

"Sorry," she breathed, then she touched him again

lightly near the wound. "You...you really needed stitches, but I'll try to pull the sides together with some tape before I put the pad on it."

Her touch disappeared, then she spoke again. "Okay, hold on. This might sting. It's disinfectant."

"Just do it," he heard himself say more abruptly than he intended.

There was a hiss and a slight cold stinging, then it was gone.

"Sorry," Shay whispered as she dabbed at his wound, softly cleaning around the edges. "There." She tore some paper, and he felt her put several bandages across the wound, before she pressed a pad over it all.

"I think that'll hold," Shay said, patting the last strip of tape.

She barely finished the sentence before Luke pushed out of the chair and turned his back from her view. He flexed his shoulder, felt the tape tug against his skin and watched as Shay collected some bloody gauze and torn packaging.

He waited for the question, for the look, but neither came. She carried the trash into the kitchen, then came back empty-handed. "You were right," she said as she crossed to the table and closed up the box of Band-Aids.

"Right about what?"

"The steps in the kitchen. Not that I counted them, but I could tell where the sink was and found the trash under it without a light."

She looked right at him. "How does it feel?"

"Okay," he said.

"Good."

He picked up the ruined T-shirt and stared down at it. He couldn't put it back on, but he wanted to be covered. Crushing the fabric in his hand, he went to the closet, dropped the ruined shirt in one of the buckets and searched for another shirt.

He pulled a towel off the shelf, then finally found what he was looking for. He barely looked at it before he pulled it on and down to cover his back. He hoped that Shay would say it was time for bed, but she surprised him.

She stood at the entry doors, her hands pressed to the glass, staring out, echoing his earlier stance. "What is it?" he asked.

"I don't know. It's so dark out there I can't see much, but the wind's starting to pick up again. It feels like this storm is never going to end."

She turned as he approached. "Um, you may want to dress again," she said and he automatically reached for his shoulder, thinking he was bleeding again, but stopped when he realized that Shay wasn't horrified. She was smiling.

"What?" he asked, baffled by her reaction.

She pointed at his shirt, and when he looked down, he understood—the damn shirt was on inside out and backwards. He looked at Shay sheepishly. "Dressing in the dark," he muttered, then tugged it off and put it back on correctly.

He wasn't prepared to hear Shay laugh, but she

did, and in some strange way, the sound lifted the tightness in him. He could see the humor, and he heard himself do something he hadn't done in what seemed an eternity—he laughed. A simple, silly thing. The sound was rusty, but it felt good.

It wasn't uncontrollable, but it was laughter. He shook his head, and managed to say, "Lesson learned."

He watched Shay as she came closer, never taking her eyes off of him. He tensed and had to force himself not to back away from her when she stopped within a foot of him. "What?" he asked.

She shook her head, and her smile caught at his heart. "I like it when you smile." Unexpectedly, she touched his chin with just the tips of her fingers, but he couldn't move.

Every emotion he'd pushed away for the past few years exploded in him. He felt need and desire, and they centered on this woman he'd known only a short time.

He was frozen. He let her draw back even though what he really wanted to do was grab her hand and hold on to her. She stepped away, and all he could do was watch her put space between them.

The moment their contact was broken, he felt disconnected, as he had in those weeks after he'd escaped. Nothing could change that now, he knew. There was no salvation for him. Not in this world.

Luke took one last look at Shay as she dropped down on the sofa, and turned to gaze at the fire. He took in the way the nape of her neck was exposed as her hair fell forward, and his body responded without warning. He quickly went into the bedroom, closing the door before making his way to the bathroom. He splashed his face with icy water.

After running his hands roughly over his wet face, he smoothed back his hair. He stared at his reflection in the mirror, but saw only a shadow of himself. He'd been alone too long. Shay's sudden appearance had proven that to him. Then her touch—the contact had been as potent as any he'd had with a woman. His body had tightened at the thought, and he knew if she'd come closer, if she'd wanted more, he wouldn't have stopped her.

He laughed roughly. And if she'd wanted more? She wouldn't want anything from him when she knew what he was. When she'd pulled away, she'd saved him from that moment when he would have seen her turn from him in disgust. When he would have seen everything that had to have been in her eyes when he'd bared his back to her. She'd saved him from that and she didn't even know it.

Chapter Nine

Shay stayed on the couch for a long time after Luke had wandered into the bedroom. Images of him looking down at her, his wound, what he'd taken to save her life, then his smile flitted through her mind. And she'd touched him. She lifted her hand and stared at her fingertips, as if she could still feel the bristle of his beard and the heat of his skin.

She closed her hand and exhaled. This was crazy. Whatever she was feeling was a product of this place, this situation and this man being the only person to talk to for the past two days. She closed her eyes, but opened them immediately when she had a vision of Luke's back, bare and strong, the wound from the falling tree…and something else. A scar. It had been pale, almost invisible, just above the waistband of his jeans, but she'd seen it.

Another puzzle piece in the larger picture of who Luke was. The man was an enigma on so many levels. He seemed harsh and withdrawn, then he'd do things like carry her to protect her injured feet, or make sure the house was warm even when she knew he hated the heat. She saw sadness in him, and hints of what the man could be if he smiled.

"It's late," Luke said, interrupting Shay's thoughts.

She looked up and saw his hair was damp. "Yes, it's late."

She stood while Luke pushed the glowing wood in the hearth farther back. She could see his chest expand with each breath he took, the way his muscles rippled, and the outline of the bandage under the thin cotton shirt.

"Luke?"

He glanced over his shoulder at her, his expression lost in the shadows. "What?"

"Is there enough wood to keep the fire going tonight?"

He turned to the hearth and studied the short stack of logs next to it. "I'll bank it for the night, then figure it out in the morning."

"Okay," she said, and started to the open door to the bedroom when Luke stopped her.

He met her halfway, holding out the lamp. "I don't need it," he said.

"Are you sure?"

"Yes," he said.

"Good night." She closed the bedroom door, and for some reason, felt very close to tears. She didn't know what was making her eyes burn as she crossed to the bed and crawled under the blankets that Luke had spread out for her. She pulled them up to her chin and exhaled. She felt for her wedding ring, and rubbed it with the tip of her forefinger. The world had gone crazy, far removed from everything she knew, and she wanted her regular life back.

The ring was smooth and cool, always there. But it didn't ease her frustration. She shut her eyes. Things would make sense when she left here. When she was gone and Luke was alone again.

She rolled onto her side, pulling her legs up to her stomach, and tried to ignore the howling of the wind and the stupid dreams that made little sense. The fact that Luke inhabited most of them made even less sense.

She stirred, waking from a crazy dream of Luke and the water, of him rescuing her. The windows shook and the chill in the air was bone-deep. Suddenly she heard something—a door opening and closing. She waited to see if it would happen again, but there were no more sounds from the next room.

She pushed herself up, staring into the thick darkness as if she could see through the door if she tried hard enough.

She was about to get out of bed to check on Luke— had he gone outside?—but she made herself stay where she was. He could take care of himself. She rolled onto her side, snugged the blankets to her and closed her eyes. The wind grew even stronger, and Shay finally fell into a soft sleep. Her last thoughts were how lucky she'd been that Luke had found her on the beach, that he'd gotten them out of the main house in time and that no man should be as alone as he seemed to be.

SHAY GRADUALLY WOKE the next morning, rolling onto her back while she listened to a strange silence in the room. There was no howling wind, no rain or hail beating on the house. The silence was heavy and complete beyond the sound of her own breathing.

She slowly opened her eyes and saw a weak gray light that barely touched the corners of the room. She couldn't see outside because of the icy frost on the windowpanes, but the storm seemed to have finally passed.

She pushed herself up and raked her fingers through her unruly curls, then stretched her arms over her head. With the storm over, she could feel her time at Lost Point drawing to an end. She knew she should feel relieved and excited to be able to get away from here finally, but she didn't. For some reason, she felt was vaguely depressed. Maybe it was just cabin fever.

Pulling one of the blankets off of the bed and tugging it around her to ward off the chill in the room, she slipped off the bed. In the living room blankets were folded and stacked on the end of the couch along with Luke's pillow. She inhaled and smelled the wonderful fragrance of coffee. Walking farther into the room, she could feel heat in the air, and when she neared the kitchen, she saw Luke, his back to her, standing at the counter by the sink. "Coffee?" he asked without turning, obviously knowing she was there.

He seemed to have a sixth sense when it came to her presence, and she never had a clue when he was sneaking up on her. "Yes, thanks," she murmured. "The storm's over?"

He stirred the coffee before glancing over his shoulder at her. His eyes were shadowed and the scruffy beard darkened his jaw. He looked tired, and she wondered if he'd slept at all during the night. "You haven't looked outside?" he asked.

"There's frost all over the windows in the bedroom," she said as he looked at the back door. "And I…" Her words died as her gaze followed his. She blinked at what she saw. Or thought she saw. The sky was gray, but the rest of the world was white. Everything was pure white. She crossed to the door and stared out at snow. It was everywhere, hiding everything except the general shapes of the land around the house. The only recognizable feature was the sound, gray and choppy off in the distance, below the bluffs.

Closer to the house, huge pines were heavy with snow, their branches bending so low that some blended into the whiteness on the ground. The deck was nonexistent, with the angles of the rails and posts changed into soft mounds of powder.

She pulled the door open, and snow that had blown against it tumbled in and onto the wooden floor. She touched it with her bare toes and shivered from the cold contact.

"My gosh," she whispered. "It's incredible."

She turned to Luke, who was watching her. "It's so incredible that it's shut down the city and all the services. If it wasn't New Year's Day, the problems would be a hundredfold."

She'd forgotten what day it was, but all she heard was that the services had been shut down, meaning she still might not get home. "That includes the ferry, doesn't it?"

"The ferry probably hasn't run for a while, and I doubt it's going to start up again very soon."

The snow she'd let into the house smeared on the floor and left traces of white, along with a series of puddles. "I had no idea that it ever snowed on the island."

"Neither did I," he said, and tossed a small towel onto the wetness.

She touched the towel with her foot, rubbing at the moisture with the terry cloth. When the floor was dry, she finally picked up the damp towel and threw it in the sink. Then she turned, spotted the radio on the counter near Luke and turned it on to hear the weather forecast.

Luke handed her coffee, and she shifted the blanket to keep it around her shoulders, then took it.

"Seattle's buried under the snow, and the airport's been shut down until further notice," Luke said. "They're short on snowplows, and with the temperature staying low, it's not going to melt very quickly."

She let the blanket fall around her feet as she cradled the mug in both hands, and leaned back against the counter. "So I guess we're stuck here a bit longer?"

"I'd say so." His expression didn't give away anything, if he was stressed about the situation, or if he didn't care. He took a sip of his coffee. "If the snow shuts down things on the mainland too long, then there'll be pandemonium."

When he turned to add a bit more hot water to his mug, she saw the shape of the bandage under his shirt. There was no blood staining the cotton, thank goodness. She didn't ask about his wound, though, because she knew that even if there was a problem, he wouldn't tell her.

"Why don't you go and clean up?"

"Good idea," he said, and took his coffee with him into the bedroom. When he shut the door behind him, Shay crossed back to the door and stared outside. The snow was incredible, and just as isolating as the rainstorm had been such a short time ago. She had no idea how long it would be before she could leave, and yet she didn't mind.

The thought came out of nowhere, and it sat there in her mind as she sipped coffee and let the heat slip down her throat. She had nothing waiting for her on the mainland, and no one waiting for her. She was stuck with Luke, and he was stuck with her. That didn't sound too bad to her at the moment.

She heard Luke open the bedroom door and come up behind here where she still stood at the door. She met his gaze in the reflection from the frosty glass.

"What's so funny?" he asked, when he saw her smile.

"Nothing, just…the snow, it's such a surprise and it's so very beautiful."

"You think so?" he asked, his focus on the view.

"Don't you?"

He blinked, then shrugged. "It's okay I suppose."

"Just okay?" she asked.

He met her surprised expression, then said, "It's beautiful."

That made her smile again. "There you go. That wasn't so hard, was it, to admit that it's really beautiful out there?"

"No, but I doubt you'd think it's so beautiful if you had to shovel it."

"*Do* we have to shovel it?"

"No, we don't. I was just saying—"

"You've shoveled snow before, I take it?"

He almost looked embarrassed by the question. "Actually, no, I haven't. I mean, I have, but not sidewalks or driveways. It was because I wanted to, not because I had to."

"Why would you shovel it if you didn't have to?"

He went back into the kitchen to make himself more coffee. He stirred it, then said, "Snow forts."

"What?" she asked as she grabbed her blanket and headed for the couch. She curled up on the cushions, pulling the blanket around her legs and cradling the mug. Luke had started the fire again, and it gave off very welcome heat.

He sat down on the chair, sipped his coffee, then said, "Snow forts. You shovel the snow to build the walls. You make the three walls three or four feet high, and if you're really creative, you put a couple of holes in them so you can see the enemy sneaking up on you."

"Were you really creative?"

"I never did it right, but Chance, he had the touch. He could make a hole in the wall big enough to see in both directions, yet the wall never collapsed."

"Who's Chance?"

The question was innocent enough, yet it made Luke blink, as if he hadn't been aware he'd uttered the name. He finally answered. "Chance was the son of our housekeeper."

"You had a housekeeper?" she asked.

"My mother didn't know how to boil water, and Mrs. Shore took care of the cooking, the cleaning and care of me, most of the time. I grew up with Chance. He was a month older than me. Always said that made him my boss."

"And you made snow forts together."

"Yeah, we sure did." He stared down into his coffee mug. "Great snow forts. Awesome designs. Chance was a natural architect." His voice was touched with roughness. "He understood angles and load stress, things I didn't even know existed, and our forts would last until the spring thaw."

"Did you have snowball fights with each other?"

That brought his head up. "Fights with each other? No, not usually. We teamed up and defended our fort from other kids. I made the snowballs, and Chance watered them down."

"He did what?"

"Put water on them. The snowballs would freeze and the ice made them go faster and sting when anyone got hit by them." He shook his head ruefully. "They hurt like hell."

"You two must have been a great team."

He sighed roughly. "We were."

"And how about now? Are you still close?"

"No," he said.

"Oh, that's too bad," she said. "I always hated losing contact with friends, but I guess growing up means growing away from people, too."

"Chance is dead," he said bluntly.

She was stung by the anguished look he shot at her, and thought that Luke had exposed more of himself in that moment than he had since she'd met him on the beach.

"I'm so sorry."

"Yeah, me, too," Luke said as if he couldn't believe what they'd been talking about. He stood, laid his mug on the side table, then said, "I'm going up to the main house to take a look around and if it's safe, will get what I can."

She stood, as well, and put her mug down by his. "I need to come with you."

He shook his head. That was the last thing he wanted her to do obviously. "No. Stay here where it's warm. I'll bring some extra wood if I can find any and grab more food, too."

"But I can help you carry things back."

He hesitated, then said, "Do what you want."

"Okay, but wait while I change." She ran into the bedroom, and before she got inside, she realized she couldn't go with him—she had her jacket but nothing to put on her feet. She went back to find Luke ready to leave.

"I can't go," she said. "I don't have boots or shoes and walking barefoot in the snow probably isn't a smart thing to do."

She thought he'd just leave, but he surprised her when he said, "I'll go up there by myself, and if I can, I'll get you something to walk in."

"Okay, but please be careful."

"That's the plan," he said and left.

She closed the door behind him, then went over to the fireplace. She looked in the wood bin and found another log, one of two that were left, and tossed it onto the fire. The flames looked good and the heat was even better. She started pacing the room, realizing she felt nervous. What if Luke went back in the house and got into some trouble? How would she know? She looked around for a clock, but there weren't any in sight.

Unable to do much else, she sat on the couch, listened to the radio and waited for the time. Nine-fifteen. She listened to more oldies than she could stand, until the announcer finally said, "Now for Seattle news at nine-thirty on this New Year's Day."

Luke had been gone fifteen minutes. Not horribly long, but long enough for him to get to the house, get inside, find some shoes or boots for her and get back. But he'd said he was going to bring other stuff with him. That would take more time. She forced herself not to go to the door and check out the main house. She just sat on the couch, watched the flames in the fireplace leap in the air and waited.

"News at ten on this cold and snowy New Year's Day." Shay stood at the announcement. She pushed the blanket off of her, and headed for the door. Forty-five minutes was long enough. Just as she opened the door, Luke was coming toward her, a holding a trash bag in one hand and a full leather wood carrier in the other.

She waited for him to take the snowy steps up onto the porch, then she reached for the bag. "You were gone so long," she said, but didn't tell him how worried she'd been.

"It's a bit difficult getting around the house when half the second story is on the ground floor."

She moved back to let him in. "Is it that awful?" she asked, leading the way into the house and into the kitchen.

"It's bad enough," he said, taking the wood to the hearth and placing it in the storage drawer.

She put the garbage bag on the floor and opened it. Canned goods, frozen food, some folded clothes and a bottle of wine. She glanced over at Luke as he straightened, looking bulky and big in his peacoat and boots. "You thought to bring wine?"

"You left the bottle on the counter last night and I grabbed it."

She brought out two bottles. "Glad you did," she

said, and started unloading the bag. Luke joined her and took out the clothes, laying them on the counter.

"A couple of shirts, jeans, and—" he reached in and came up with a pair of rubber boots "—I found these in the utility room. Don't know whose they are, but hopefully they'll fit you."

"Thanks," she said, taking them to try them on. They were big on her but, all things considered, not too bad. "Perfect."

She kept them on while she finished putting the food away, then she turned to Luke. "Ready for a second trip?"

"If you're up to it."

She folded the green bag and left it on the counter. "Ready."

"Okay." Luke headed back to the front door.

She ran for the bedroom, the boots slipping but staying on her feet. She put her jacket on and did it up on her way back to where Luke was waiting for her.

He opened the door, stepped outside, and she went after him. She shoved her hands in her pockets and hunched her shoulders against the wind that attacked her as soon as she got to the porch stairs. The oversized boots were loose, but she was careful when she got to the porch stairs. Careful not to slip out of her oversized boots, she stepped into the tracks Luke had already made in the calf-deep, virgin snow.

They headed through the blinding whiteness and cold to the main house, climbing onto the side terrace that was almost hidden by one of the trees

that had fallen in the storm. Snow covered everything, and as Shay looked at the house, she thought
at first that it reminded her of some oversized
witch's cottage. The trees seemed to embrace it until
she saw the roof that had been crushed under their
weight. The whole center of the house dipped down,
the windows were cracked and some were gone
completely.

The side door was ajar, and Luke slipped inside.
It wasn't until she did the same that Shay realized that
the door was open because the ceiling had collapsed
on it, jamming it in that position. Luke turned to her
before she could do more than take a few steps. "No,
don't come in. Stay there."

She looked past him, then met his gaze. "I don't
think anything's going to collapse. If it were going
to, it would have under the weight of the snow last
night. And you've already been inside."

"That's my choice."

"It's my choice, too, and I want to come in."

"God, you're stubborn," he said, but didn't fight
her anymore. He turned away and passed through the
utility room into the next room. She followed, and
with horror surveyed what was left of the kitchen. A
smaller tree had smashed through the area on the far
end, caving in the ceiling to her right. It was as if the
small room beyond it had never existed.

Cracks ran along the ceiling, and tiles from the
backsplash and counters were shattered on the floor.
"Be careful where you step. Stay near the inside

walls, and away from the windows. One exploded when I was in here getting the clothes."

Her eyes met his. "Okay."

He went through the dining room, past the once elegant table that was now covered with plaster dust and burled wooden ceiling tiles. One leg had snapped.

Luke walked along the inside wall of the great room to get to the entry hall when Shay stopped and couldn't smother a soft cry at what she saw.

She pressed both hands to her mouth to muffle her shock at the sight of the fireplace where she'd been sitting when Luke had returned to get her. A huge tree had crushed the wall of windows and the French doors, and one of its main branches had landed on the hearth, reducing it to rubble. Pine needles and snow seeped through holes in the wall and ceiling.

"Don't look at that," Luke said, but she couldn't turn away. She stared at the scene, the image burning into her mind. If Luke hadn't persisted that she leave, Shay could have been killed.

She started to shake, and Luke got to her just before her legs buckled. He caught her, drawing her to him, and the trembling got worse. "Hey," he soothed as he held her. "Shay, it's okay. You're okay."

Chapter Ten

Luke held Shay close, and despite what seemed like a lifetime of avoiding touching anyone, he didn't want to let her go. "You're okay," he repeated.

"No," she said, her voice muffled against his chest. "If you hadn't forced me to go outside, to do what you asked me to do…" A tremor shook through her. "God, I could have died. I was right on that couch by the fireplace. You…you really did save my life."

"Shay, no—"

"I can't believe…" She choked on her words and simply stopped. She was crushing his jacket in her hands, holding on to him for dear life.

Luke eased her back, but didn't let go of her. He looked down into her pale face. "Don't do this. Don't go over what-ifs or could-have-beens."

"You saved my life," she said in a voice so unsteady he could barely understand the words.

"You keep saying that, and I've told you it was nothing. I acted on instinct."

"No," she said, her eyes overly bright. "Don't do that. It was more than…" She touched her tongue to her lips. "You're a hero."

Her words tore at him the same way they had the first time she said them. Lucas Roman wasn't a hero. Never had been. Never would be.

"If I've learned one thing, it's that life is as unpredictable as it is crazy. We can't count on anything. This time it worked out. Sometimes it doesn't. We were lucky."

She trembled again. "I know," she murmured. "Graham was there one minute, gone the next. No reason, not really. Just gone." She shivered violently, and he gathered her to him, letting her curves fit into his angles. His chin brushed the top of her head and her hair tickled his skin.

"I'm sorry," he whispered and meant it. She'd loved her husband, and if there were heroes in this world, he just bet her Graham had been one. Compared to him, Luke didn't measure up at all. And that made his chest ache in the oddest way.

Shay tipped her head back, and he found himself looking into those amber eyes again. Her lips were parted, and when her tongue touched them, he couldn't breathe. She lifted her hand to his cheek, warming it with her touch. "You…you have to learn to accept thanks," she whispered, then before he could stop her, she stood on her tiptoes and touched her lips to his.

There was silky heat and unsteadiness in the

contact. He felt her breasts against his chest, her hand brush his neck, before it came to rest on his shoulder. Letting the moment just be what it probably was meant to be, a kiss of gratitude, was shattered. Maybe if she hadn't smelled so good, or if he hadn't heard her small sigh of pleasure, he would have stopped it. Maybe. But he didn't.

His hands lifted, framing her face, and he tasted her mouth. He connected with her on the most basic level, and the chaos around them no longer existed. There was just Shay. Her body against his. Her lips under his. Her softness and warmth under his hands.

His head spun, and he knew that all he wanted right then was this woman. Someone he had no right to want. Someone he had no right to need. But he did.

Her tongue met his. He lost every bit of restraint he could have mustered when he felt her hands sliding under his jacket. Her hips pressed to his, and he knew that she understood how much he wanted this. There was no way to hide his arousal. She fit against him as if she'd been born just for this, and a hunger exploded in him that bordered on desperation.

Her hands moved to his waist and under his shirt, and he froze when her fingers touched his back. But she didn't stop. She caressed his muscles, and her lips trailed away from his mouth to his throat. She was trembling and he figured he was, too, but all he knew was she wasn't pulling away from him. His heart beat so hard against his chest he could feel it.

Then he remembered the man she'd been with.

Graham. Perfect Graham. Luke couldn't go up against that memory. He didn't stand a chance if she knew the truth. Besides, she deserved so much better than anything he could offer her.

It was the hardest thing he'd ever done, but he pushed her away and, looking into her eyes, he lied. "No," he said. "No, this isn't a good idea."

He saw color rise in her cheeks, and the way she blinked at his words, then she dropped her gaze and stumbled out of his reach. She tugged at her jacket and pushed her hands back in the pockets. "Sorry," she mumbled and went back the way they'd come. He didn't go after her. He simply watched her until she was out of sight, then he uttered a curse that shook him.

He wasn't a hero. He never was, but ending what he knew he could have had with Shay had been the most noble thing he'd ever done and it made him sick. He couldn't remember why he'd come in here and didn't bother trying to figure it out.

He returned to the kitchen, found another sack and stuffed more food from the refrigerator and freezer into it. He stopped by the wood pile, got as many logs as he could manage to carry, then hooked the bag over one arm and started for the guest house.

Shay was nowhere in sight, but he didn't miss her footsteps in the snow, which were a good five feet from the path he'd made earlier. He felt his stomach drop, then he trudged back to the guest house.

SHAY HEARD LUKE come back, but she stayed in the bedroom. She'd stripped off her jacket and the loose boots, and had been sitting on the bed, staring at her hands and wondering what sort of desperate idiot she was. First she'd almost had a breakdown seeing the damage to the house, then she'd kissed Luke.

She closed her eyes and put her head back against the headboard. She'd kissed him. For heaven's sake, she'd kissed him.

She heard the door, and listened to Luke as he crossed the room and put down something with a muffled thud. She didn't move. She couldn't go out there and act as if she hadn't suddenly become some desperate widow who kissed the first man she met who saved her life. She laughed at that, then slapped a hand over her mouth to muffle the sound. Hysteria was far too close to the surface for comfort.

A knock sounded on her door, and she remained where she was. "Yes?"

The door opened and Luke peeked in. "If you put the food away, I'll stoke the fire. It's getting low."

He was talking to her as if nothing had happened, and she could have cried with relief. If he could pretend that she hadn't embarrassed herself, so could she.

She scooted off the bed and followed him out into the other room. Luke was at the hearth, and she put away the food he'd brought, then turned on the radio. She was sure the batteries were going to go dead anytime now. All she heard was music, and she almost turned it off, then the news came on.

There was more talk about the snow, about the accidents and businesses that had closed. The airport was full of stranded passengers, but there were hopes it would be up and running by early next morning.

She shut off the radio after hearing it was just after noon, then joined Luke by the fire.

He sank back on his heels and watched it. "I'll try to figure out what we can burn later on for heat in case we run out."

"Isn't there more wood at the house?"

"Can't get the rest of it," he said without turning.

"Why not?"

"One of the trees shifted and that part of the house took the brunt of its weight. I was halfway back here when I heard the groan and turned in time to see the tree take out the side door. There's no way to get to the wood now."

She felt sickened that she'd been so blithe about the situation, saying it was safe to go in the house, that it wouldn't get worse. She bit her lip. "How about furniture?"

He shrugged. "If it comes down to it."

They were talking about things other than her ridiculous behavior, and she didn't know if she was happy about that or not. Why hadn't he questioned her actions? Because it hadn't meant much to him. He'd only been trying to comfort her when she got hysterical.

Shay knew she should have been thankful for his silence, but she didn't feel thankful at all. Now he was telling her that they might use the furniture from the main house for fuel for the fire.

"The fire feels great," was all she could think to say.

He crouched in front of the hearth, resting his forearms on his thighs. "I don't care much for fires. I used to, then I was in a place for a while where there was nothing but heat. Day and night."

He stood slowly, and turned from the leaping flames. "We won't go back to the main house," he said.

She cringed. Here it came. But he surprised her when he spoke and his words had nothing to do with the kiss.

"It's not worth the risk and there's nothing there we can get to. It's off-limits."

"I can't imagine how your boss will feel when he finally gets to see his poor house."

Luke gave her a "whatever" look and said, "I brought enough coffee to last us for a while."

She turned and thought of the rest of the day that stretched out in front of them. She wished there were some books around, or even a deck of cards. "You don't suppose there are any games around here, do you?"

He cast her a slanted look over his shoulders. "Games?"

"Yeah, a deck of cards, checkers or chess set."

He shook his head. "I don't know." He nodded to the house in general. "See what you can find. You never know what you might turn up." He reached to turn on the radio to hear the weather update and added, "And if you find some batteries, it wouldn't be a bad thing. Or more oil for the lamp. They're both getting low."

The small house was so spare that she doubted she'd find any surprises, but she decided to explore anyway. When she got to the last set of drawers in the kitchen, the radio began to fade, and before she or Luke could get to it to turn it off, it died.

"My kingdom for some batteries," she muttered as she went back to finish looking in the last two drawers. "Or a bottle of oil." But she found nothing. "No luck," she said as Luke came out of the bedroom.

He was tugging his T-shirt down over his flat stomach, and he paused just inside the room when he saw her. "No batteries?"

She shook her head. "Nothing at all." She looked past him into the bedroom, and saw the only drawer she hadn't looked in before.

Making a beeline for the nightstand, she opened the drawer in it. She found a stack of writing paper, two pens and an unopened deck of cards. "A minor success," she called to Luke.

She held up the deck of cards. "Unopened. They won't give us any light or get the radio back on, but if we're here long enough, I could leave rich."

He lifted one eyebrow. "How do you plan on doing that?"

Ripping the plastic off the package, she slipped the cards out of the box onto the side table in the living room. "By winning any money you've been hoarding over the years." She grinned.

He looked down at the slick new cards scattered on the table, then his dark eyes met hers. A shadow of a smile lingered at the corners of his mouth, and she just wanted to remember it.

"I have money? No, no cash to speak of, but how about an IOU? And I doubt you've got any money with you, considering the way you arrived."

She shook her head, and pulled her distorted wallet out of her jeans pocket. She took out five one-dollar bills and a twenty that she had dried since her swim. "Twenty-five bucks, and I'm good for, maybe, double that."

Then a real smile sprang to his lips, a smooth, easy grin that touched his brown eyes and her heart. "Big spender," he murmured.

She turned to pick up the cards, then tugged the small table so it sat in front of the couch. She sat down cross-legged, and avoided Luke's gaze as she spoke. "Your IOU is like cash to me. I trust you to pay your debts." She would have shuffled the cards, but realized her hands were less than steady. She put the deck on the table and nudged it in Luke's direction. "Pull up the chair and sit down, then shuffle."

"There you go, bossing me around again," he said as he did exactly what she'd told him to do. "Cut," he ordered after shuffling the cards.

"So name your poison," she said when she finished.

"Anything but hearts." He chuckled, and the sound was like velvet.

She had to swallow before she managed to say, "How about poker?"

"Draw or stud?" he asked.

"Draw."

"What's the ante going to be?"

"A dollar?" she said, and took out one of the crumpled bills and dropped it on the table. She finally looked up at Luke, who was methodically shuffling and reshuffling the cards, but his eyes were on her. "Where's your ante?"

He placed the cards on the table, and went into the kitchen, returning with a half roll of paper towels. He tore off three pieces, then proceeded to rip those pieces into several one-by-one squares. He laid them in a pile and picked up one, then dropped it on her dollar bill. "Each one is a dollar," he said, then dealt out five cards each facedown.

"How come I don't get to make my own money?" she said.

He tore off three sheets and handed them to her. "Knock yourself out," he said. "But you have to mark yours."

She copied what he had done, put the pile beside her and marked an *S* on each slip of paper. She glanced at her cards, then did a double take. Three queens and two sixes.

"Okay, I check," she said to Luke as she tried to act nonchalant about her full house.

He narrowed his eyes on her, glanced down at his

own cards, then added three pieces of paper from his stack to the pot.

She picked up four of her own and put them in the pile. "See you and raise you a dollar."

He leaned back in his chair, then tossed his cards onto the table, facedown. "I've got a feeling I'm walking into a trap. It's all yours."

She grinned at him. "Good decision." She laid her cards down face up. "A full house." She gathered the pot to her. "I feel riches coming on."

He gave her a crooked grin which was more endearing than any expression had the right to be. "Don't get too confident," he drawled, and pushed the deck toward her. "Your deal."

For the next few hours, Shay could have almost believed that she and Luke were good friends, passing a snowy afternoon in front of a fire, playing cards and talking about nothing much at all. But with each passing moment, she felt herself falling into a place that truly had no spot in reality, at least in the reality of her life. A time out of time. She wanted to remember the way Luke would cock his brow when he studied his cards. When he did that, she knew he had a good hand. Or the way he'd lightly tap the table with his forefinger. When he put down his cards, they inevitably would beat anything she had.

When Luke had most of his "chips" in front of him, along with twenty-two of her twenty-five dollars, and a quarter of her paper, he said, "Last hand, and I'll let you double the value of what you have left."

She eyed him, taking in every angle and plane of his face. She barely noticed the scar through his eyebrow anymore, and the lines at the corners of his eyes looked more like laugh lines now rather than signs of stress. She wasn't sure when he'd mussed his hair, but she could see more gray in the strands than she remembered.

She looked down at the three dollar bills in front of her and her feeble amount of paper remaining. "Double or nothing?" she asked.

He chuckled. "Be my guest."

She dealt the cards, then picked up her hand without looking at it. "Okay, who's first?"

"Me," Luke said, then played.

She stared at her cards for a long moment—an ace and four number cards that didn't match and were of different suits—then tossed five paper chips into the middle. Luke took his time, then matched her bet. "How many?" he asked her.

She took her time, then said, "Oh, I think I'll take…three."

"Three? Well I have hope," he murmured, and asked for two for himself.

She took her three, and he drew his two, then he waited for her bet. She glanced at her miserable hand, which was no better than it had been before the draw, then put in her remaining pieces of paper and sat back. "It's your move."

He matched her bet and raised five.

She stared at him, but his face was unreadable.

"Okay," she said. "My turn." She finally picked up five more chips and dropped them in the middle. "It's up to you."

He looked from the pot to her, then down at his cards. She was sure he'd fold and she'd win. Then he stunned her by pushing all of his "money" into the center. "All in," he said.

She stared at him, then exhaled and tossed her cards onto the table, surrendering. "How did you know?" she asked.

He actually looked as if he was gloating just a bit. "You're so damn easy to read," he joked and took the pot.

God, she hoped not, or he'd know that she was feeling her heart skip at his voice, or that she only had to look at his lips and remember his taste. No, she hoped he'd never know what she was thinking.

LUKE COULDN'T REMEMBER the last time he'd looked at a woman and wished he were someone else— anyone else. Or when he'd had to concentrate on the cards in his hands to avoid staring at the sweep of a woman's throat when she looked up, or thinking about how he'd love to place a soft kiss there. Or when he'd deliberately tried not to look at the way a woman's breasts rose and fell with each breath she took.

"How am I easy to read?" she asked.

How *wasn't* she easy to read? She touched her nose with the tip of her forefinger when she was thinking, and she tended to lean toward him when she was earnest or excited about a hand. "You've got your tells," he said.

"Do not," she countered quickly. "I was deliberately trying not to give away anything."

"I'd advise you not to quit your day job," he said as he picked up the cards and started to shuffle them.

That brought a grin from her that seemed to light up the room. "I guess I shouldn't ever become a spy, huh? My enemies wouldn't even have to torture me to get the national secrets out of me."

Her words hit him out of left field, and the cards slipped from his grasp, flipping up into the air, then scattering on the table and the floor. Luke pushed away from the table so quickly that his chair toppled backward onto the floor. They had been simple words. Words that she had no idea meant a thing to him. Yet they'd ripped him wide-open, and he was trying desperately to stop them from playing over and over again in his mind.

He dropped to his haunches, reaching for the scattered cards. Shay tried to help, their hands tangling as they both made a grab for the same card.

He jerked back and accidentally upset her balance, propelling her toward him. With the impact, they both went sideways, and he hit the floor on his back. She fell onto him, and the next thing he knew, she was straddling him. Her hair tangled around her face, and her lips were so close that he knew all he had to do was lift his head a few inches to taste her again.

Before he could do anything, though, she scrambled off him.

He could hear her soft breathing, the shuffling sounds as she paced. Then she came back extending her hand to him.

"Sorry about that," she said, and he ignored her hand to roll to one side and push himself up. If he'd touched her, he wasn't sure what would have happened. Better to just make no contact at all.

He turned and Shay was picking up the last of the cards. He didn't bother to help.

When she was finished, she put them on the table, but didn't look at him. "Don't think I've given up getting rich off of you. How about upping the ante to two dollars a hand?"

He didn't want to sit across the table from her right then. "I need some fresh air. I think I'll take a look around, and see how the house has settled."

She turned to him quickly when he spoke. "You aren't going back inside, are you?"

"No," he said quickly. "I told you, it's not safe. I'll just check the outside."

He thought she'd suggest coming with him, but she didn't. She sighed. "I'll make something for dinner while you're out."

Her comment was so mundane, but he knew that she didn't want to be close to him any more than he wanted to be close to her.

"I'll be back," he said on his way to the door. He

put on his boots and jacket, then slipped out into the cold and whiteness.

He took his time trudging around the house, seeing more damage than he'd first suspected. He figured about five trees had toppled, probably one after the other, as the ground weakened each time roots were torn out. The house, as far as he could tell, would probably be a total loss.

He came around the front as the daylight began to fail. Pristine snow was everywhere, hiding the driveway and banked high against the gates in the distance. It would take a plow or a sudden change in temperature to make this place accessible anytime soon. Shay wouldn't be leaving for at least a few more days. And they'd be stuck in the little house all that time. They could play cards. They could sit and stare at the ceiling, but they'd be alone.

Chapter Eleven

Luke passed the massive stone arch that designated the main entry, and it looked remarkably intact. The trees had done their damage beyond it. He could see small cracks in the heavy windows above the entry. He was sure Maurice would want to rebuild and probably duplicate what had been there to maintain the value. Luke didn't care. If the place had to be leveled, it wouldn't matter to him. Without Shay, loneliness would take on a whole new meaning.

"Luke?"

He saw her come around the side of the house by the terrace, bundled up in her jacket and wearing the oversized boots with the jeans tucked into them. He waited where he was, until she was almost up to him.

"What are you doing out here?"

She stopped in front of him, and when she spoke, her breath misted in the cold air. "I needed some fresh air, and to be honest, the snow is so pretty, I wanted to walk around in it a bit. I might not get another chance, especially not in San Diego, and since my assignments tend to be in warmer climates, I don't expect I'll see snow again for a very long time." She glanced at the house and grimaced. "It's odd how something so beautiful can be so destructive," she mused.

"That's pretty much life," he said, and looked up at the sky and the heavy clouds still hanging over them. "We might get more. I doubt it can do much more damage to the house, but I'm glad you can enjoy it."

"We could build a snow fort."

He glanced at her, thinking she was teasing him, but she looked serious. "I never said I wanted to build more snow forts."

"What would you like to do then?"

He shrugged his shoulders and pushed his hands deep in the pockets of his jacket. What did he want to do? There was no way he would tell her what he was thinking. It was bad enough he could barely pull his eyes from her lips. "Get back inside," he said, and started back to the guest house.

She kept up with him, then said, "You know what I always wanted to do in the snow?"

"I can't begin to guess," he muttered without stopping.

"Make a snow angel." She stopped somewhere behind him. "You need perfect snow for it, or so I was told."

"There's plenty of—" He turned and saw Shay standing about ten feet behind him, arms outspread, and suddenly she fell straight backward into the snow. When she landed, she started sweeping her arms and legs back and forth. And she was laughing. No, she was giggling.

Luke looked down at Shay lying in the snow, and her arms and legs stilled. She grinned up at him as if she was a little kid who'd hit the jackpot. "Isn't this incredible?" she asked.

He stared at her. "Incredible," he echoed, but he wasn't talking about the snow, or the angel she'd made. Shay Donovan was incredible. He'd known her only days, yet she'd done something that no one had been able to in years—she'd lightened his heart. She gave him a reason to smile, and if he were honest, he was actually grateful she'd ended up on his beach and that a storm stranded them. "Really incredible," he said.

Shay sat up and held her hands out to Luke. "The tricky part is getting out of here and not messing up the angel."

He stood there as if too dumb to realize she wanted him to pull her out, but truth was, he was literally afraid to touch her. He remembered the way her hands had felt on him as she'd stroked his back, and he had to brace himself before helping her.

She took both his hands in hers, and although the contact was cold and damp, it seemed to sear him. He tugged and she easily came up and stumbled forward, leaving the form of the angel she'd created in the pristine snow.

She looked up at him, and the smile on her face faltered. Her hands tightened on his, and he thought for one stunning moment, she was going to kiss him again. Then it was gone.

"Thanks," she breathed and released her grip. Feeling awkward, he plunged his fists into his pockets.

"I wish I had a camera," she said, admiring the angel she'd made.

He wished he had a camera, too, so when this was over, he'd have proof that he hadn't lost his mind. That he hadn't imagined this woman and the time he'd had with her. Just one picture. One thing to hold on to.

He resumed the hike back to the guest house, and hesitated before going inside. He finally turned and saw that Shay was nowhere behind him. Luke was sure she'd joined him and immediately he was concerned about where she'd disappeared to.

He looked right and left into the dusky afternoon. "Shay!"

She didn't respond at first, then he heard her voice at the same time he saw her footprints heading left through the snow.

"Be right there," she said.

He barely ducked in time as a snowball sailed past him to hit the porch. She lobbed another one at him, and this one hit home, striking him in the arm.

He ran to his left, across the porch and behind a snow-covered shrub. He grabbed a handful of snow, pressed it into a hard ball, then cautiously peeked out and around the shrub. A snowball missed his head by inches.

"Dang," he heard her say. From the direction of her voice, he knew she was hidden behind the hedge that lined the walkway to the stairs that went down to the beach.

He tossed one snowball toward her, then took off the opposite way. He jogged as fast as he could, back and around the house, skirting the side, then crawling under the supports for the deck.

He slowed down, moving silently and faced six-foot drifts against the side of the guest house. As he formed another snowball, he inched toward the hedges. He heard soft breathing, then when he was within a couple of feet of his target, he saw Shay stand. She was holding a snowball and aiming it right at him.

Laughing, she nailed him in the chest and the force pushed him backward into the pile of snow behind him. Suddenly Shay was over him, her arms raised in the air in triumph and he knew he'd never wanted a woman as much as he wanted her.

He looked up at her, and his own laughter came in a burst. He laughed so hard he barely felt the snow going down his neck, or the coldness seeping through the legs of his jeans. He laughed so hard that he gasped for air, and for that one perfect moment, he loved life. He loved everything about what was happening, and if things had been very, very different, he knew that he could love this woman.

SHAY DIDN'T HAVE a clue why she did what she did, except she wanted to have some fun with Luke. She hadn't wanted to return to the house yet. She wanted to enjoy her snow angel and to enjoy it with Luke. Now, standing over him, all she could think of was how happy he seemed. Their laughter came in waves and echoed around them.

She bent to offer her hand, and he took it. As she started to pull him up, she figured an apology wouldn't hurt anything, either.

"I'm sorry," she gasped around her giggles. "I just thought…who needs a snow fort?"

His fingers closed around hers, and instead of getting to his feet, he pulled her down to him. She landed on top of him, her body next to his in the snow.

Their breath mingled, and she lifted a hand to touch his lips. His dark eyes held hers as his tongue touched her finger, then he kissed it. Fire flared in her belly, and she knew she should pull back. She should get off of him. She should get up and go inside and try to ignore what she was feeling, the way she had ignored the kiss they'd shared in the house. But she didn't. She lowered her head and found his lips with hers.

At first he returned the kiss, but then he stopped and gently pushed her away. Once on his feet, he offered his hand to her and lifted her as if she were as light as a feather. She stumbled to get her balance, but he never let go of her.

He pulled her to him, cradling her in his arms, the way he had the first night, but she wasn't fighting it now. She wrapped her arms around his neck and pressed her face into the roughness of his jacket. He carried her with ease up the porch steps, and he kicked open the front door. Once inside, he set her down, and she didn't take her eyes off him.

She wasn't sure what she thought she'd find in his expression, but it wasn't the sadness that was there. His eyes were filled with something she thought could be regret, but she wasn't sure.

"What?" she breathed.

He shook his head, moving past her into the room. "This isn't right," he said.

She stared at him, speechless. "What's not right?" she asked.

He turned. "Me."

"Luke, no, please." She pushed the front door shut and stepped out of her boots. "I didn't mean to kiss you out there. At least, I don't think I did." Now that was garbled at best.

She tugged off her jacket, tossed it on the floor and made herself go closer to the man. "I really am sorry. I don't know why…" That was a lie. She knew why she'd kissed him. She knew very well what had driven her to do it. But she couldn't tell him. "It's me," she finally said. "It's me being alone and…" God, she felt sick. "I'm sorry."

"No, it's not you." He went to the couch and dropped down on the end. Sitting forward, he buried his head in his hands. "I have to tell you something about me." His hands dropped and his eyes met hers.

"And after I tell you, it's okay to just walk away. I would if I were you."

Her chest tightened and she sat on the other end of the couch, partly because her legs felt weak, and partly because she knew that getting closer to Luke was wrong. It wouldn't solve anything. "You don't owe me any explanations," she said softly.

He shook his head, then raked his fingers roughly through his hair. "I damn well do."

She almost flinched at his tone, bit her lip watching him. She could see the tension in him—his jaw was taut and his hands curled into fists so tight his knuckles were white.

"What is it?" she asked, praying she wouldn't regret saying those three words.

He took a ragged breath, then started in a low voice. "Chance and I enlisted in the navy at the same time. We did everything together. Brothers couldn't have been closer. We grew up together, went to college together, decided to drop out together and signed up for duty together."

Why was he telling her this? She'd thought he was going to say he was married or something like that, and she'd hoped that wasn't the case.

Before she could ask him anything, he continued. "After training, we were assigned to the same unit. Since we weren't technically family, the navy didn't have a problem deploying us together, and they knew Chance and I worked well as a team.

"Chance had a wife and two boys. I know it was

hard on him leaving them, but he never complained until that last time. That was when he told me that was it, he was getting out. He'd put in his time, but he wanted to be with his family."

He hesitated, then spoke as if his past was running through his mind. "It was our last assignment together, a simple one actually. Go in, find the contact who was in place, give him the intel and get out. But, we never made it to the contact. We never made it," he repeated.

"We almost made it to the spot, and some stupid city official called us out. I never knew how we'd been made, but we didn't stand a chance. They took us in broad daylight. The locals watched, and a few clapped when the 'infidels' were taken away.

"They drove us to a small village, and that's where I saw Chance for the last time. He was pulled out of the car by two men dressed in black from head to foot, and he actually smiled at me and said, 'See you soon.' That was it. 'See you soon.' And then he was gone.

"They took me to a house cut into a hill, put me in a room with no windows, a single light overhead, a stinking blanket and a hole in the ground. I was there for almost nine months."

"Luke," she said softly, and it took all of her will-power not to take him in her arms and comfort him. His eyes were on the floor. "You don't have to—"

It was as if she wasn't there. He kept talking and she couldn't do a thing but listen. It broke her heart to hear about those nine months—the darkness, the heat, the pain and misery. Never knowing if anyone even knew he was still alive. Never knowing what happened to Chance. Never knowing if he himself was going to live or die.

She felt helpless, especially when he told her about a nightmare that he carried with him when he finally escaped.

He told her about the day he'd had an opportunity to escape, that he took it, the rope burns on his back, the scar she had seen. How that represented so much of what he hated. He'd believed he'd die before he made a break for it, but he hadn't cared by then. He'd gotten away, walked barefoot for miles before he stumbled on an American patrol officer who almost shot him when he thought Luke was the enemy. Luke had been taken back to safety where he told his story and found out that Chance hadn't survived. They'd found him four days later on the side of the road, dead.

"Luke," she said softly when he was finished. She inched toward to him. "Please, stop. You don't have to—"

He finally looked at her, as if he just noticed she was still there. "I came back," he said in a whisper. "Chance didn't. The group who took us got the information they wanted."

After what he'd told her they did to him, she didn't question his breakdown. Most men wouldn't have survived something like that. "You aren't to blame for being human."

He exhaled. "Human? I'm not sure I am," he said.

"I was let go from the navy with a discharge that was as vague as it was forced. But people got the idea. They accused me of treason."

"After what you went through?"

"They had to think something. Men were lost because of the information I gave to the enemy."

"What about Chance? He was there, and he—"

"He's dead. He left two sons and a wife. And their boys know that their dad was a hero."

"And what about you?"

Luke had said words he'd never expected to utter in this life again. The last time he'd talked about this had been at his debriefing. Until now.

Since meeting Shay, he'd pushed away the truth of his past. She'd felt like that lost part of him, but when she'd kissed him outside, he knew he couldn't lie to her any longer. He had to tell her who he really was. His fear that she'd turn away from him now was even greater than anything he'd experienced before. But she was still here. She stayed beside him, and her hand was on his arm.

"What about me?" he echoed. "I survived. I didn't have a family to worry about. My dad's dead, and my mom more or less sort of disowned me when I enlisted. There is no one else." *Until now*, he thought, but didn't say it out loud. "I got out and finally just disappeared. I came here."

"And you're still beating yourself up over what happened?"

He never thought of it that way. He'd just separated himself from other people, people who would look at him as a curiosity, as a traitor, as a man who went against everything he'd promised to uphold.

"I did what I did, what I had to do."

"And what about Chance's family? Do you still see them?"

He hadn't seen Jenny and the boys since those first weeks he'd been back in the States. Jenny had looked years older than she should have, and the boys' sober expressions never should have been seen on children five and seven years of age. But they had the memory of a dad who'd been brave and who had died a hero. At least they had that. And Chance's pension would help Jenny and the boys when they really needed it.

"They wouldn't want to see me," he said truthfully. "I hear about them from my attorney. He keeps an eye on them. But, no, I haven't seen them for a long time."

She exhaled softly and her grip on his arm tightened. "I am sorry, so very sorry for everything you went through over there, and when you got back. You deserved much better."

He didn't want her sympathy or pity. "So did Chance."

She touched her fingers to his chin, urging him to look at her. He could barely meet her eyes. "So do you," she whispered, then leaned toward him and kissed him again. She wasn't turning away from him or disgusted with him. But he didn't have a thing to offer her. And she deserved the very best.

The kiss tore at him, but any thoughts of being noble, of pulling back, of doing the right thing, fled when she stood and grabbed his hands. "Luke."

He ached for what he'd never known and for what was right in front of him. He stood and her mouth found his again as her arms circled his waist. The completeness he felt in his soul was staggering, and he knew that even for a short time, he wanted that. He wanted to hold it to him and never let it go.

SHAY HAD NEVER WANTED to touch someone the way she wanted to touch Luke. What she felt for him was different from what she'd experienced with Graham. This was new, and she wanted desperately to reach out and heal Luke. To ease his pain, and to just plain love him.

Then he had her in his arms, carrying her to the bedroom. He set her down by the bed, standing in front of her with his hands at his sides.

"I want…" he started to say in a choked voice, but the words wouldn't come. He swallowed, then cleared his throat. "I want you."

She wanted to say, "I want you, too," but was so overwhelmed that all she could manage was a nod.

He touched her face, and his hand was as unsteady as she felt. "Are you sure?"

She nodded again, then almost fell against him. His arms encircled her and she clutched his shirt. She was afraid that if she moved, this would all dissolve.

Luke would be gone. And she didn't want that. She wanted him here with her, making love to her.

Luke lifted his hands, framed her face and tipped it so she was forced to look up at him. When their eyes met, any restraint was gone. They pulled at the clothes that separated them. He tugged her shirt up and off, tossing it to the floor. Shay couldn't wait, either, and pulled at his shirt. Skin against skin, Luke took her to the bed.

He stood over her for a moment, looking down at her, and with a gentleness that brought tears to her eyes, he finally lay beside her. Body against body. Heat mingling with heat. She'd tried to shut off her feelings for so long, but they were as clear as anything had been in her life. This man had rescued her again.

She felt as if she'd broken through a fog that had been her life for the past two years, and into a place where she was living again.

Luke lay his hand against her hip, then cupped her bottom to pull her closer to him. She felt his hardness against her, and she gasped her need for him. His fingers worked their way under the waistband of her panties and eased them down. Then he touched the center of her, and she arched toward him.

Nothing prepared her for the instant pleasure she felt at his touch. She tugged at his underwear, freeing him from the confines of the cotton material. She explored him with her hands, and felt his hardness under her touch. He gasped, and pulled her more tightly to him.

He shifted up on one elbow; his mouth traced a path from her lips to her throat, then down lower to her breasts. He slipped off the flimsy bra so he could suckle her nipple. She almost cried out. Pleasure shot through her and she arched toward him, holding him as close as she could.

His hand moved lower, to press between her legs. He found her, and his finger was in her. "Yes, yes, yes."

She grabbed him by the shoulders, digging her fingers into his skin, holding on to him as if her life depended on it. And she knew that it did. If he let her go right then, she was certain she'd just drift away, that she'd leave this man and this place and never be able to find her way back to either.

He continued to caress her, and she could feel the knot forming in her middle, that aching need that begged for release.

She spread her hands on his back, and lower to his waist, then she felt the faint ridge of the scar there. At that moment, the world stopped. Luke's hand stilled, and she could feel him retreating. She opened her eyes, and he shook his head.

"Luke, it's all right."

He hesitated for a few seconds, but it felt like a lifetime to Shay before he said, "I'm no good for you. I've got nothing to give, and you deserve so much."

That was so far from the truth that she couldn't even begin to tell him. "No," she said, and felt tears burning her eyes. "You're…I want you," she whispered, and when he turned away from her, she caught him by the arm. His back was partially to her and she acted on instinct. Leaning toward him, she touched the scar on his skin with her lips. He trembled as she touched his bandage on his shoulder. He'd gotten that by helping her, and it would leave a scar, too. It only made her want him more.

She pulled him back to her, forcing him to look at her. "I need you."

Her tears rolled down her cheeks, and he reached out, fingertips brushing away the moisture. "Yes," he said simply and kissed her.

She never took her eyes off his face as he pressed against her, testing her, then with aching slowness, entered her. She lifted her hips toward him, and when he started to move, she met each thrust, going higher and higher. When she felt she couldn't absorb any more pleasure from Luke, she climaxed. She cried out, her voice mingling with his.

The world narrowed to the two of them, that moment in time when they were one, and she wished with all her heart that it wouldn't end, that this would go on and on forever. But soon, she felt herself drifting back to reality. Luke turned them both onto their sides, holding her close. Their faces were inches apart, and neither one looked away. Shay memorized every line in his face, every imperfection, then kissed him, and snuggled into his chest.

She wouldn't think of tomorrow. She wouldn't sort through any of this. In the morning she'd figure

it all out, but until then, she was here with Luke and
that was all that mattered. She felt him take a shuddering breath, then sigh, as if something in him had
been released.

Chapter Twelve

Luke felt as if the weight of the world had been lifted off him, thanks to one touch from Shay. He held her, not believing she was still beside him, and knowing that his time with her was short. He couldn't ask her to stay—he wouldn't—but when she kissed him, when he tasted her and their breath mingled, his need for the woman overwhelmed him. His need for her burst inside him, flaring from deep in his soul, and he knew that one thing he'd learned since Chance's death was to live in the moment because you never knew what would happen tomorrow.

He shifted, framing her face with his hands, tangling his fingers in her hair and kissing her as if his life depended on it. And it did. He felt whole with her. He felt alive and complete.

He kissed her hard and long, as if her touch could mend his wounds.

She responded to his kisses, straddling him and pressed against his hardness. He held her waist and lifted her just enough for him to enter her.

With her hands on either side of his shoulders, she lowered her body and leaned forward. Her full breasts brushed his chest, as potent an aphrodisiac as anything he'd ever experienced.

Together they blended into one, and when they climaxed, Luke lost himself in her. He treasured their lovemaking, wanting to remember every nuance. He pulled her down against his chest, and stayed inside her as long as he could. He closed his eyes, and felt a peace he thought had been lost to him forever. Although he knew it would never last, right then he wasn't ready to let it go.

THEY MADE LOVE AGAIN during the night, long and leisurely, savoring each touch and each caress. Later they lay in the shadows, talking or just holding on to each other. When Shay finally drifted off, she felt his heat against her body and snuggled into it. When she woke, it was to an empty, cold space beside her.

Taking a quick look around the room, she soon heard noises in the living room. It sounded as if Luke was taking care of the fire. She tried not to think, not wanting to remember anything except loving him in every way she possibly could.

Love? The possibility was there, and she considered it, knowing that love was different for everyone. She held up her hand to look at the slender gold band still on her finger.

She'd always thought that you had one chance at true love in this life, and had accepted that Graham had been that once-in-a-lifetime-love. But now Shay realized how wrong she'd been. Loving Luke didn't diminish what she'd had with Graham. What she'd had with Graham had been wonderful, if short. She would never forget him or what they'd meant to each other. But it was time for her to stop grieving and to live again. She touched the smooth gold band and smiled.

"I'll always love you," she whispered, then slowly slipped the ring off her finger. She looked at the perfect circle, then closed her hand around it, knowing she'd just finished another chapter of her life. Saying goodbye to Graham would be challenging, but she was ready to take that step.

She pushed herself up in bed, letting the blankets fall. Quickly, she grabbed her clothes and dressed. She pushed the ring into her pocket, then headed for the door.

Luke was crouching by the hearth, his back to her. She felt a surge of hatred that almost choked her. Whoever the nameless, faceless men who hurt Luke were, she'd never understand or forgive them for what they'd done. Luke stood and turned, and she felt the extreme opposite emotion when their eyes met. Love flooded through her, and she smiled.

"Good morning," she said. For a moment, she felt awkward, but then he wrapped her in his arms.

She tipped her head back, wanting and needing to say the words in her heart. *I love you*, topped the list of things she wanted him to hear. She was about to say it when Luke stopped her. As he framed her face in his hands, she felt him tremble.

"Shay, we have to…" He took a breath. "We have to talk."

"Sure. Of course," she murmured.

"What we have between us, we can have for now, but when we can get you back to town, it's over."

His words stunned her, and she pulled herself from his grasp. "What?"

"This here, now, us—this is all there is." He motioned to the room. "It's all there can be."

She shook her head. This wasn't right. It couldn't be. Not after loving him the way she had. "But, Luke," she started, not sure what to say or how to say it. "It can't just be…" She couldn't just walk away after all they'd been through. She couldn't. "Luke, that's crazy."

He came closer to her, cupped her shoulders. "What's crazy is me letting this happen, and wanting it to happen, knowing that it can't last."

"Why not?" she asked.

He shook his head and closed his eyes for a long moment as if bracing himself, then his dark gaze was on her. "I have nothing. *I* am nothing." Pain touched his expression and it made her ache.

"No, no," she whispered, lifting her unsteady hand to touch his cheek. "No, that's not true. I don't care about your past or what you did. It's gone and I don't care."

His face tightened. "I do care and you will."

"Luke, please, don't do this."

He sighed. "You'll never know what your being

here means to me right now, but there's no point in exploring whatever is happening between us after we get out of here." He closed his eyes.

She'd never expected to have to make a choice like this. She hated it. And for a split second she hated him. "How could you?"

"That's just it, I can't. I can't be what I'm not." He suddenly leaned down and kissed her fiercely. "All we have is right now. That's all I can offer. If it's not enough...?" His voice trailed off, but he kept his hold on her.

Not enough? Forever wouldn't be enough with him, yet she knew about having only the moment. But maybe, if they had time, she could make Luke see that a future was possible.

She pressed her hand to his heart. "All right, just now. Just here. You and me until this ends."

He lowered his head to hers and kissed her with a passion that made her want to cry, then they were back in the bedroom, making frantic love, savoring what they had.

For the next two days, they were together, and Luke didn't mention their bargain again. They talked about what their lives had been before they'd met, and she was stunned to find out that he was the elusive owner of Lost Point. She told him about her childhood, about her parents and about being alone now that Graham was gone. She told him things she hadn't thought about for years, and she held to him, only letting him go to get them food, or drinks, or so they could sit by the fire.

On the third morning after the New Year's Eve's blizzard, Shay woke with a start.

"Sorry. Dropped a log," Luke called.

Shay sank back in the pillows. "I'll get breakfast in a bit," she called back.

Shay took her time getting up and putting on her clothes. Luke was still tending the fire when she came out. They were down to just a few logs, then the antiques would have to go. "Good morning," she said with a smile, loving waking to find Luke here.

He straightened and approached her. "Good morning to you, too," he said, and hugged her to him. "Look. The snow's starting to melt."

She turned in his arms and looked out the back door. He was right, the level of the snow was decreasing and she could see water running in rivulets off the roof. While she knew she needed to get back to her life, a part of her was sad to know that when the snow melted, her time with Luke was over. She turned back to him as her heart dropped just a bit.

"Maybe there'll be another storm," she said, not adding she was hoping for one.

"The sky's clear," he murmured, then kissed her and let her go.

For the first time since he'd told her that what they had was over when she could leave, she felt that separation between them. As if he were building space to make her departure easier, and she hated it.

She started to go to him as he sank down on the couch, but was startled when a heavy banging sounded on the door.

"Hey," someone shouted, banging on the barrier again. "Is anyone in there?"

Luke looked at the door, then back at her and the gulf between them grew wider. "I guess the cavalry has arrived."

Shay wanted to stop him from saying anything, from opening the door and letting the world in, but she didn't get a chance. He was already up and at the door.

Two men stood on the porch—a tall, balding man in a heavy plaid jacket and a shorter, heavy man wearing what looked like a police uniform. The shorter man did all the talking.

"Oh, thank God you're in here. We saw that house, and good grief, it looked pretty bad." He saw Shay behind Luke and nodded to her. "Is everyone okay in here?"

"Yes," Luke said. "Just no electricity or heat in here, and the main house…it's about done."

"Yeah, it looks as though it needs to be leveled," the taller man said. "Those old trees can get pretty unstable and with all that wind and rain, then this snow." He shrugged his wide shoulders. "It's been a real crazy start to the new year."

Shay thought the men would leave now that they knew no one was injured or in trouble, but that didn't happen. The policeman startled her by saying, "Would either of you have seen a woman in these parts named Shay Donovan? Her boat was adrift in the sound and she called to let the coast guard know about it a few days ago. She was supposed to call them back, but no one's heard from her since. The Agency she works for have been calling to find out what was going on. We traced the 911 call to this place. We've had a hard time with the snow and all, but we finally got here."

Shay went forward, impervious to the cold drifting in the open door. "I'm Shay Donovan. The phone's been out, so I couldn't call them back."

The policeman smiled at her. "Well, little lady, no matter. We're just glad you're okay, and we're here to get you out of here so you can get back to the mainland. The coast guard found your boat and have it all snug at impound. Now you just have to get back to let them all know you're okay."

Shay didn't care about the boat, but knew she had to contact the Agency. She turned to Luke, but he was avoiding her gaze. "She'll be ready in five minutes," he said to the men.

Shay had let hope live in her up to that point, hope that Luke would realize they could be together. But at his words, she felt her stomach bunch. "I need some time," she said to the men. She looked at Luke, "I need to talk to you."

He barely glanced at her, but the policeman spoke up. "Take your time. We're in the Jeep on the other side of the front gates. We couldn't get them all the way open, but managed to squeeze through a gap between them. Just come on out when you're ready. We'll be waiting with the heater going."

"Thanks," she said, and Luke swung the door shut as they left.

When he turned to her, her breath caught in her chest. The lover from these last days was gone, and the man she'd first met, the man behind the wall, was back. She searched his face for the softness she seen, and there was none.

He said, "It's time for you to go."

Shay knew that dying from a broken heart was impossible, but the pain in her soul felt deadly to her. "Luke," she said, forcing herself to not reach out to make sure he was real, to make sure she wasn't hallucinating and this was all a horrible nightmare. "I can't just leave like this." She wanted to say more, but stopped.

For a second she thought he reacted to her words, then it was gone as if it had never been. "I told you, you have to. You can't stay and you agreed," he said. "There's nothing here for you. You're safe now, and you can go."

She felt as if she'd been punched in the stomach. It was all she could do to not double over with the anguish, but she found enough strength to look him straight in the eye. She swallowed, then ran a hand over her face. The words *I love you* were there, but she kept them to herself.

"Is this what you really want?" she asked in a hoarse whisper.

He closed his eyes, as if he didn't really want to look at her, then nodded. "Yes."

Shay could barely breathe, and she felt everything slipping away from her. "But, Luke, we—?"

"It's over. It's done." He shrugged as if he'd said a movie had ended. "We had a deal. This was a fantasy—a great one—but it's over."

She wanted to scream that loving him wasn't a fantasy, but she didn't. She'd never say those words to him, and she was grateful that she hadn't. She'd been rescued, and those men would never know just how they'd saved her from something she couldn't begin to imagine. "Sure," she whispered.

She hurried over to find her jacket and was shaking so badly she could barely get her arms in the sleeves. As she went to the front door, Luke moved back to let her pass. She was ready to walk out, when Luke spoke. "Shay?"

She turned, a faint glimmer of hope still alive in her. "Yes?"

"Take the boots. You can't go out in bare feet."

She shook her head. "What do you care?" she muttered, all the hurt and bitterness rising to the surface.

"Don't be childish. You can't walk through snow in bare feet."

She stared at him, so thankful she wasn't crying. Her eyes were painfully dry now. "I can do whatever I damn well want to do," she said, and turned to walk into the icy cold with her bare feet because she could. And she wouldn't take those damn boots.

But that backfired when Luke suddenly reached for her and picked her up. "Then I'll carry you," he said in a flat voice.

He walked out of the house with her in his arms, ignoring her struggles to get free and the cursing that came out of nowhere. She hated his touch as much as she'd begged for it last night. She hated the feel of his breath on her face, and the sound of his voice in her ear. "Calm down, dammit."

He carried her through the snow, ignoring her demands to put her down that were turning to sobs. She finally stilled as they passed his truck covered with snow.

She closed her eyes to avoid looking at anything, especially Luke.

"Goodbye," he said and she realized she was already outside the gates, beside a huge yellow Jeep. The back door swung open, and Luke lifted her up and into the car.

She almost tumbled inside, then righted herself as the door was closing. Before she could say or do anything, the bald man who was driving, said to Luke, "Thanks, and we'll be back to check on you until the electric's up and running."

Luke said something before turning away and heading to the gates. The bald man backed up the Jeep, and Shay sank back in the seat feeling as if she were lost again, as lost as she'd been when she'd fallen overboard. But this time, she felt as if she'd lost her way home, and she'd never get there again.

The big vehicle backed up slowly, and as the driver did a U-turn to head into the town, she looked at the gates. She wished she hadn't.

Luke stood there, his hands in his pants pockets, watching her leave. Then he was gone. It was as if he'd never existed. Shay hugged her arms around her middle to try to ease the growing pain there.

"Bet you'll be glad to get back to the mainland," the man in the plaid jacket said as he looked at her over his shoulder.

All she could do was nod, knowing it was a lie.

One month later

SHAY CLOSED her notebook and turned off the light in her cubicle at the agency.

"Hey, there." Startled, she turned to see Rafael Luna, the man who had hired her, a short, swarthy man in a rumpled gray suit—grinning at her.

"Hey, yourself," she said, picking up her books and papers. "I was going to come by to see you before I left."

The middle-aged man smiled at her. "Same thing I was doing. I wanted to thank you for everything, and to say how sorry I am that you aren't going to stay longer. I'd love to give you an extension, especially now that we have the clearance to look on the beaches at Lost Point more thoroughly."

She glanced down at the desk, as if checking to make sure she hadn't forgotten anything, but was trying to settle herself at the mention of Lost Point. She tried not to think about Luke at all, but that was a pretty hopeless feat for her. All she had to do was look out the window and see Shelter Island, and Luke was there. Luke standing on the bluffs, in the storm, in the snow. In her bed.

She shook her head. "I'm sure things will work out now that you can get a closer look there, and I have an offer to work for a few months in Florida."

Rafe laughed softly at that. "Well, if it was a choice between this crazy weather up here and Florida, all you'd see would be my tire tracks on the way to the airport."

All that mattered to her was that Florida was on the opposite coast from this place. "It'll be good to warm up."

"We can't talk you into staying on permanently? We don't pay much, but you'll never be bored and it's for a good cause." That was supposed to be a joke, she guessed. Falling overboard and roughing it through fog, a rainstorm and a blizzard, definitely wasn't boring. "And maybe, in a while, we could come up with a bit more in the money area to tempt you to make it permanent."

She took one last look at the office, then out the window at the island in the distance draped in late-afternoon fog. If things were different, she would have thought long and hard about staying here permanently, but she was still missing the piece she wanted most.

"I appreciate the offer, and I'll think about it." But she knew she'd never come back to this area.

"Sure, maybe you'll get tired traveling, or get bored in Florida, and when you do, think of us, okay?"

"Yes, I will," she agreed, and put on her jacket over jeans and a white tunic, then walked down the hallway with Rafe. They parted in the parking garage with hugs and good wishes, and she drove out onto the street clogged with afternoon traffic.

She didn't cry much anymore, and she thought about how close grieving for what might have been came to grieving for a permanent loss. With Graham, his leaving had been final, not his choice. With Luke it *had* been his choice, and as long as she knew he was out there, losing him didn't feel final at all.

Her schedule had been laid out for her, and after the flight back to San Diego, she needed to tie up some loose ends there before flying to Orlando.

Despite her plans, nothing was settled; she was unable just to let go of what happened with Luke. She needed closure. She hated that word, but now she understood it completely. She needed an end she could accept.

Turning away from the direction of the airport, she put in a call to cancel her ticket and have it left open for later, then drove toward the ferry docks.

She was sick with nerves, but didn't hesitate taking the ferry across the choppy waters of the sound to Shelter Island. The thing was, once she got to the island and drove toward the town of Shelter Bay, she was nauseous and having trouble convincing herself that this had been a good idea. She clearly wasn't a fly-by-the-seat-of-her-pants sort of girl. She'd impulsively let herself love Luke and look how that turned out. But she had to see him one more time. And if he told her to leave, if she couldn't convince him that all she wanted and needed was him, she would. She was stubborn, but even she knew when she was beaten.

Five minutes later, she drove into the town that had been obviously styled to complement the pirate lore the island was famous for. Bartholomew Grace had left his stamp in more ways than one.

She made her way along the main street, then stopped by an open coffee shop next to an old-fashioned town square, down to and including the white gazebo fronted by a brass statue of the pirate.

She got out and went inside, ordered her coffee, then sat down by a front window to look out at the late afternoon streets.

The girl who sold her the coffee came over to her table and offered her a refill. "Thanks," Shay said to the tiny red-haired girl who couldn't be more than sixteen or so. "It's good coffee."

The girl hesitated. "Anything else?"

"I heard you had snow over here when that New Year's Eve storm came through."

The girl smiled at her. "We sure did. It was fantastic." Then she sobered a bit. "I mean, there was trouble, you know, and some people had their houses damaged, but no one was hurt and it melted pretty quickly. We didn't miss any school because of it." She frowned, clearly disappointed by that last bit.

Shay thought about the house on Lost Point and the collapsed roof. "I heard that some houses were worse for the wear."

"Oh, yeah, they sure were. Old man Sloan's place just buckled in the winds. Nothing to do with the snow, but it just sort of gave way. He'll have to redo the whole thing, which isn't all bad since it was pretty messed up to begin with. Then there was a place at the far end that got all messed up. Some landmark to do with Bartholomew Grace. Some people around here are pretty upset that a bunch of trees fell on the house. It was built a long time back, then it was fixed up and real fancy, from what I heard. But it's pretty bad now. The good thing is, no one got hurt."

No one got hurt? Not so it showed, Shay thought. There were no outward scars, but they were there all the same.

Shay stood and said, "I think I'll take this with me."

"Have a good stay on the island," the girl called after her as Shay carried her coffee out to her car.

Shay sat there for a long time, halfway thinking she was a fool and should go back to catch the next ferry and get whatever flight she could get to San Diego tonight. She shook her head. If she was a fool, so be it. One thing Luke had said hit its mark—you only have now. This moment in life. The future together wasn't promised, but she hated living this way day by day.

She headed north out of town and toward Lost Point. She'd been here twice before she'd landed on the beach where Luke found her. But unlike the other two times, she wasn't here to see the elusive Mr. Maurice Evans.

Amazingly, the snow was totally gone, but she could see where the vegetation had been frozen and killed by it. Tree limbs lay on the side of the road where they'd snapped off during the storm, and as she got farther north, the road had scattered debris on it. The cleanup efforts hadn't extended quite this far yet. She slowed and spotted the driveway that cut straight off the road, went back a hundred feet and stopped at the closed gates to Lost Point.

Chapter Thirteen

Shay left the car idling and got out to approach the closed gates. They were solid, but where they met, there was a gap of a couple of inches. She looked up the drive and saw the house. Now without the snow, there was nothing magical about it. It looked like a war zone to her. The roof had collapsed in the center, and chunks of the side had fallen to the ground. Several windows were shattered and the downed trees hadn't been cut up and moved. She couldn't see the guest house from here, but everywhere she looked, the place seemed empty. There were no signs of life anywhere.

She pushed on the gate, but it didn't move. Then she saw a hasp on the other side that probably was fastened with a lock. She couldn't get in this way.

She moved back and looked around. She'd come this far, she was going to at least find out if Luke was still here. It hit her then that he could have left. He could have just walked away from everything, but she had to know.

She pulled her navy jacket around her against the growing cold and headed north. She followed the fence until she reached the bluffs and stopped at the very edge.

She grabbed the last support post and managed to reach around it to the other side. Gripping a wire that tangled near the ground, she pulled herself up and ended up on the other side within inches of the twenty-foot drop to the beach below.

She backed away from the cliff and looked up at the house far to the right, then at the trees by the guest house, where she then headed. But as she approached it, she could sense it was deserted.

She took the steps in one stride onto the porch, then knocked on the door.

"Luke?" she called, but there was no response. She tried the handle and the door swung open silently. He still didn't lock doors.

"Luke?"

She looked inside, the living room as sparse as when she'd been there. No fire burned in the hearth now, and the back door was shut. She slowly entered, memories assaulting her from everywhere. She stopped and one last time called out, "Luke?"

Her voice echoed back to her and she was alone. She stood there, then forced herself farther inside. Everything looked the same. She went to the back door, opened it and glanced out onto the deck. She half expected to see Luke there, in his shirt and jeans, his feet bare and the wind tangling his hair. But the deck was empty, too.

She closed the door, then crossed to the couch and sank down on it. She was motionless, knowing she should get up and leave, admit defeat and go, but she couldn't. She'd stay just a bit longer, then, if Luke didn't come back, she'd head out and she'd never see this place again.

THE ENTRANCE to the agency where Shay worked was brightly lit in the dusky light of the late afternoon, and Luke found a parking spot right in front. He stopped the rental car he'd picked up at the airport and sat there, staring at the doors. It was just after four, and he could see people milling about inside. Three days ago he'd left the island for the first time in two years and gone back into the real world.

At first the chaotic noise had assaulted him, and people seemed to be everywhere, then he realized that no one was giving him a second look. The name "Lucas Roman" didn't raise any interest at the car rental desk or at the hotel where he'd stayed in Virginia for two nights.

He'd contacted Maurice Evans, found out where Chance's widow lived and, without calling, flew out to see her again. Luke didn't know what sort of reception he'd expected, maybe her screaming at him for leaving Chance behind, or not even acknowledging his presence at her front door.

He hadn't expected Jenny to hug him so hard he

could barely breathe. And he sure hadn't expected to be introduced to a nice guy in navy blues who shook his hand and welcomed him into their home. Jenny and Derek had been married six months, and Jenny had tried to let Luke know, but she hadn't been able to find him.

The boys—bright, happy kids—had come home from school and shown him a picture of Chance taken about six months before he'd been captured. Chance Junior had looked at Luke and in all seriousness said, "My dad was a hero." In that moment, Luke knew that no matter what the cost to him, staying away from Jenny and the boys had been the best thing he could have done for everyone.

He'd stayed for a short while, then excused himself, saying he had to get home, but wanted to stay in touch. Jenny had walked him out to his car, given him another hug, then stood back and said softly, "You will never know what it means to me to know that Chance had you at the end. That you cared so much about him, that you…" Her voice had choked and she'd swiped at her eyes as if mad to have tears so close to the surface.

"Thank you," she finally said. "I know what your admission cost you, but the boys have their dad's memory intact and I'll always be grateful to you for that."

Jenny knew the truth. He thought then that maybe she'd always known that it had been Chance who broke. She'd never said, never even hinted at it. But she'd known, and that was okay.

He'd told her he wanted to stay in contact, and she said they would. Then he'd left, feeling oddly settled, yet on the other hand, restless and uneasy.

As he'd driven away from Jenny's house, Luke thought about her and her new life, and he envied her. He didn't have that option to start over, and he never would. When he'd sent Shay away, he'd burned that bridge and there was no way he could rebuild it. He didn't have the tools.

Since she'd been gone, he'd learned the real meaning of being alone. He was as alone as a person could get and still be living. Everywhere he looked at Lost Point, Shay was there. He'd hated himself for what he'd said to her that last day, but he knew she needed so much more than he could give her. She deserved so much better, and she never would have left of her own will.

But once she was gone, his life had fallen apart. He still ached when he remembered the look in her eyes when the two men had been driving her away. He hated it. When he'd made contact with Jenny, he'd needed reassurance that the life he led had some meaning, no matter how alone he was now. But instead, he'd realized that a life that was empty had no meaning at all. And his life was so damn empty.

So when he'd landed at the airport, before he headed for the ferry, he found himself searching for the agency where Shay worked. It wasn't until he was pulling up to the main entrance that he realized what he was doing. He wanted to tell Shay that he wanted the best for her, that she needed another Graham in her life, not a damaged man who had no future.

He studied the glass-and-metal building with a huge blue wave sculpture over the double glass doors. In the lobby he could see two walls of aquariums and a woman sitting behind a huge desk in the back.

A short man tugging on his overcoat came out. He hurried down the street to get into a waiting taxi.

Ten more minutes passed, and Luke finally made himself put the car in gear and drive away. He wouldn't go back there again.

He drove to the ferry, took the last trip to the island and took the south turn, driving onto the highway that circled the island. He drove slowly, almost reluctant to go home. There was nothing there waiting for him. Maurice would have left by now. He'd stayed at the bed-and-breakfast in town while Luke had visited Jenny, saying he'd get some bids on the restoration of the house.

Luke finally turned a curve in the road and swung left toward the entrance of Lost Point. It was almost dark and he hadn't flipped on the lights of the rental car. He didn't see the car parked in front of the gates, until it was almost too late.

Standing on his brakes, he barely avoided a collision as his car dipped nose down, coming within inches of a black sedan he didn't recognize.

He sighed with relief, then got out and went to check out the other car. No one was in it, and when he tried the door, it was locked. He looked up and down, but there was no one in sight, and the gates were completely closed, blocked by the two cars. He went back to his car and hit the button to open the gate. He locked his car, took his keys and walked through the gate.

The house was a monstrously twisted version of what it had once been. He half expected to see some insurance inspector looking it over, or someone evaluating the repairs, if Maurice was bothering to do it all. Luke hadn't cared as long as he was left alone in the guest house. Besides, he was thinking of finding another place to live. Somewhere away from here and the memories.

He turned and saw a light on in the guest house. He was almost certain he hadn't left any on when he'd left. Maybe Maurice had ended up staying there after all; Luke had offered it to him.

He jogged across the snow-damaged lawn, up the porch steps and approached the door. He couldn't hear anything as he reached to turn the knob. The door swung open and he saw the single light by the couch on. He stepped in, then stopped in his tracks.

Shay. She sat on the couch, her head down, and she held something in her lap. Her hair was loose and falling forward to hide her face. The sight of her brought such joy and such dread he couldn't move for a moment. He almost turned and left. He wasn't sure he was capable of seeing her and losing her one more time. But he couldn't go back.

He said her name softly as he approached her. "Shay?"

At first she didn't move, and he could see she had a box on her lap, a box he recognized immediately. Maurice had given the business-paper-sized box to Luke just before he'd moved to Lost Point two years ago. He'd never opened it. Maurice had said, "When you're ready, look at who Lucas Roman really is."

Luke had never wanted to know what was in the box, so he'd put it in the cupboard in the utility room at the main house. He remembered bringing some things down here a while ago and that box was obviously one of them.

Now Shay had it, and she slowly looked up at him. She'd been crying, her lashes spiked from tears, and he wondered why he hadn't been able to remember how very beautiful she was. Her chin quivered, and she bit her bottom lip as if to control herself.

"What are you doing here?" he asked, not daring to touch her as he so desperately wanted to do.

She glanced down at the papers she'd been going through, and with just a cursory look, he knew what they were. Newspaper clippings. Legal papers. His statements at the court martial. His life in black and white. A picture of him and Chance when they'd been kids lay on top of everything. "You…your name. It's Lucas Roman, isn't it?"

He'd told her much about himself, but now she was seeing firsthand what the world believed of him. This was it. He could barely meet her eyes. He couldn't put a name on the emotion he saw, but the closest he came was misery. It was over, really over. He felt crushed under the weight of what she knew.

"You let the government think you were the one who broke, who told them everything they tortured you to find out?"

Those amber eyes never left his face, and he told the lie one more time. "I was the one who cracked," he said.

She lifted the picture and held it up to him. Her hand shook, but she didn't seem to care. "This is you and Chance?"

"Yes," he said.

She lay the picture back in the box, then unexpectedly reached out and took his hand in hers. The contact was so startling that he jerked back and took a step away from her.

She put the box down, stood and came toward him. She was a blur to him, an unfocused version of herself. And he didn't want her to see him clearly. He didn't think he could stand that any more than he could stand her touching him when he couldn't have her forever.

But she came close, so near that he couldn't ignore the frown lines between her eyes as she studied him. "You took all that torture," she said softly, a single tear rolling down her cheek. "You took it, and you never told them anything, did you?"

"Chance is dead," he said so matter-of-factly that his voice seemed foreign in his own ears.

"Yes, he is, but you aren't."

He felt as if he were dying right then. "He was a hero."

He waited for her to walk out or to scream at him that he was no good. But she didn't do any of those things. Instead, she said softly, "You did it, didn't you? You took the blame. You let them think that you were the one, but you never did anything but care about your friend. You never did anything." She took a shuddering breath.

"And that's why you think you have nothing to give me. You gave it all for Chance. And you'll never tell the truth to anyone. You'll take all the blame and think that you aren't worthy of anything good in your life. But you're wrong. You're so wrong."

Hearing those words from her broke something in Luke and every barrier he'd put up began to crumble. He turned and blindly walked to the front door. He pressed his forehead to the cold glass.

Shay lay her hand on his back and whispered, "You did what you had to do. And no one else knows but you and me. But don't you think that Chance would say you deserved to be happy, to be free of this misery? Don't you think he'd know what you did and love you for it? That he'd hate to see you shut off and lost because of him?"

He could barely think. "Chance is…dead."

"You're alive, and you're the real hero. Not in the eyes of the world, but that doesn't make it any less true."

He turned, and Shay touched his face, then pulled

him into her arms. She buried her face in his chest, and he rested his chin on her head. He could feel her sobbing now, and for the first time since he'd been a small child, he cried, too. They held each other, and he felt as if the emptiness around him was being swallowed up by this woman's touch.

He kissed her hair, then found her lips and the saltiness of both their tears that mingled there. "You saved my life," he whispered to her.

She circled his neck with her arms and let her head fall back so she could look up at him. "Then we're even. You saved me, and I saved you right back."

Their tears stopped and a warmth spread through Luke. He brushed at the wetness on her cheek, then found he could almost smile. "I went to the agency where you work today."

"Why?" she whispered.

"I don't know. I just found myself outside the building, waiting to see if you'd come out. The whole time you were right here. Why did you come back?" He had to know.

"The truth?"

"Absolutely." He could take anything now.

She actually looked scared for a minute. "Because I love you."

He stared down at her, biting back his first instinct to tell her she couldn't love him. He didn't deserve her love. He'd never be the man Graham had been. He could never come close. But all he said was, "Why?"

"I didn't really know until I was back here,

looking at the papers and that picture of you and Chance. Then I knew I loved you because of who you are and what you are, and because you're a true hero." He wanted to deny that, but she didn't let him. "Why did you go by the agency?"

"The truth?" he asked, echoing her.

"Absolutely," she parroted.

"I had just flown in from Virginia." She looked puzzled at his statement. "That's where Jenny and the boys—Chance's family—live. I went to see them, and found that she's remarried and the boys are crazy about the guy." He took a breath. "Jenny knew about what happened. I don't know how, or when she found out, but she knew, and she thanked me. She said the boys had their father's memory and that meant, everything to her."

"See, what you did was the right thing."

He brushed at an errant curl that lay on her forehead, then said in a low voice, "Jenny had it all, and I knew that I had nothing without you. I think I just wanted to see you one more time to know you'd been real."

"That was it? Just see me, walk out and walk away?"

He felt tremor go through him. "Then? Yes."

"And now, don't you think that you deserve what Jenny found? That you deserve a life, and to be loved?"

He cupped her chin in his hand. "I didn't, until now."

She beamed up at him, then she was in his arms. He lifted her and she wrapped her legs around his hips as he walked with her into the bedroom. He hadn't slept in here since she'd left, but now he didn't hesitate. They tumbled onto the mattress together. Luke looked down at Shay and he realized he was home. He belonged. He belonged with her. Wherever she was, was home for him.

Then she smiled up at him, caressed his cheek, and said, "I love you, Lucas Roman," and he really was at home.

Epilogue

One year later
New Year's Eve

Shay sat in the guest house at Lost Point, and watched the fire in the hearth. The flames leaped and crackled, and the heat that enveloped her was delicious. She snuggled into the couch, her legs tucked under her, and she finally heard what she'd been waiting for—footsteps on the deck that sounded over the soft patter of rain on the roof. Then the door opened, and Luke was there.

She ran to him before he'd closed the door, and was in his arms, not caring that his peacoat was damp and his hair had raindrops clinging to it. "Welcome home," she said after she kissed him.

"Sorry I'm so late," he said. "But Maurice has some curator who's an expert on the homes of Bartholomew Grace up at the house, and the two men are like schoolkids planning the restoration."

Shay looked up at Luke. "But it's not even Maurice's house," she said.

"That doesn't matter," Luke said, taking off his coat and not caring that it fell to the floor. He lifted Shay into his arms and she wrapped her legs around his hips. He carried her toward the bedroom, talking as he walked, and stopping for a kiss here and there. "He's the one who found this place. He feels he has an investment in it." He closed the bedroom door with his boot.

"What about us? Don't our adventures in that place count for anything?"

Luke laughed and she loved it, almost as much as she loved the man himself. "I guess almost getting killed in it doesn't qualify as an investment."

"Almost," she whispered. "Almost."

Luke put her down and glanced at the champagne and flutes she'd put on the bedside table. They both ignored it as they each undressed the other, then fell naked into the bed. There was laughing and touching, then soft gasps and murmurs before they came together with an urgency that had been there from the first time they made love. Shay marveled at the need she felt for Luke, for his touch, for his smile. She knew she'd never get enough of it, and she didn't want to.

Content, they lay in each other's arms. Shay kissed Luke's chest and snuggled into him.

"So, I went to the agency today, and Rafe was working on some tide charts. He's really happy with the findings I got from the beach down by the ferry dock. The high levels of contaminants are still a mystery, but they're dropping. He's sending the samples and the screenings to a lab in Atlanta. He thinks they can track down the culprit."

Luke lifted himself on one elbow, and his hair fell forward. He kissed her quickly, then pulled back. "You're so damn good at what you do. First you figure out that the problems up here were from the oxygen cycle, and now this?"

She ran a hand down his stomach and he laughed, but the sound was a bit shaky. "You're good at everything you do," he said in a rough whisper.

Since they'd married six months ago, Luke had changed. He was relaxed and more open. The nightmares had stopped, and he'd actually started going to the mainland with her off and on. When she worked at the agency, he met with the firm that ran his family investments, and for the first time, he was getting involved in them. Then they'd take the ferry back home, close the door and just be together.

She'd gone to the city alone today, but couldn't wait to get back. Unfortunately, Luke had been tied up at the house with Maurice, even though it was New Year's Eve. But now she had him all to herself. She needed to tell him what to expect in their new year, but she wasn't sure how to start. "When they get the house restored, do you suppose that you'd want to live in it?"

He lay back and exhaled. "I've thought about it, but it's so damn big. Seven bedrooms and six baths. I'm not sure about the square footage, but it's a lot.

Old Bartholomew liked his space, even when he was hiding out licking his wounds. I'm not sure that I want a place like that anymore. Besides, this place feels like home."

"I love this place, but the main house could be terrific. You aren't hiding any longer, and as far as too much space, we could use it."

"How? Take in boarders? Or rent out half of it to a marching band? No, it's way too much room for the two of us."

She tried to think of another way to tell him her news, but she was at a loss and ended up reaching to turn on the radio by the bed. The oldies station was on, and Luke chuckled when the DJ said, "Just fifteen minutes to midnight, and here's a question for all you lovers on this New Year's Eve." The music started a soft version of "What Are You Doing For the Rest of Your Life?"

"Spending it with you," Luke whispered to her.

She stroked his chest lightly with the tips of her fingers. "Absolutely, and since we got married and we've been so lucky with a second chance for both of us, we should share the main house."

He covered her hand with his, pinning it over his heart, and she closed her eyes. "Shay?" he said through the shadows. "What are you talking about? Why are you so taken with the main house suddenly? You haven't even been in there since the trees were cleared and the renovations started. Well, except to get wine out of the cellar."

"The wine's good," she said, "and I found a particularly wonderful bottle of champagne for later." Realizing he was never going to figure out what she was trying to tell him, she took a breath before plunged in feet first. "How about sharing it with a child, Luke—with our child? You never said anything about it, but you're so crazy about Chance's kids, and they love you. When we went there after the wedding so I could meet Jenny, even she said you'd make a terrific father."

Luke sat up and turned away from her to sit on the edge of the bed, and for one horrific moment, she thought he would head for the door and keep going. She scrambled to her knees, touching his shoulder where the wound had healed, and she kissed him there. He didn't move.

"Okay, it's okay. It was just an idea," she said quickly, but he didn't speak. He didn't turn to look at her, either. At least he didn't leave.

She retreated, sitting back on her heels. "I just thought that…" She stumbled over the words, then blurted out, "I love you so much, and I'd want nothing more than to have a family with you, but if you don't want it, just say so. It's okay as long as we're together."

He slowly turned to face her. "You never said you wanted a family," he said in an unsteady whisper. "You've never said anything about it, and…" He touched her bare shoulder, then leaned forward and kissed the curve of her neck. "I think that a child with

you would be one of the best things I could do in this
life besides loving you."

She framed his face with her hands. "God, I love
you so much."

He gathered her to him, and they fell back in the
bed. She twisted so they were side by side. "We'll tell
Maurice that he can do the house, but he has to in-
corporate a nursery into the plan. That should give
him a timeline to shoot for, and when it's done in a
few years, we'll be ready. Meanwhile," he said as he
cupped her breast in his hand and teased her nipple,
"we can practice and practice and practice."

She laughed, her heart so full she could barely
contain her happiness. "Trust me, Luke, you don't
need any practice," she said. "And you'd better tell
Maurice to make the nursery a priority. We'll need it
in about seven months."

His hand stilled. "What?"

"Seven months. After I talked to Rafe today, I
went to see the doctor. I've been so tired and had no
appetite. Turns out I'm not sick, and I'll be feeling
fine in about seven months. You'd better plan on
being the only one to drink that very expensive champagne I put on ice."

Luke looked stunned, then a smile spread across
his face as his hand lowered to cover her stomach.
"Did I ever tell you that twins run in my family, and
that they skip a generation?" he asked in a voice
bursting with emotion. "My father was a twin, and
since I'm not, that means…"

"There could be two little Lukes running around in that huge house." She liked that idea very much and glanced at the rain-smeared windows. "When it snows here again, you can teach them how to build a snow fort and make great snowballs."

He kissed the top of her head and whispered, "A snow fort with holes in the walls to see the enemies so we're always safe."

"Yes, yes," she said softly. "And when they're old enough to really understand, I'll tell them about how you found me on the beach and saved my life."

He traced her lip with his finger. "And how you saved me right back."

The radio exploded with the sounds of the new year being welcomed—the music, the horns and the laughter. Shay snuggled closer to her husband as the rain brushed the windows and his heat mingled with hers. "Happy new year," she whispered, and Luke showed her how very happy every new year would be with him.

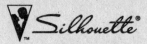

Silhouette®

Romantic
SUSPENSE

Sparked by Danger,
Fueled by Passion.

When evidence is found that Mallory Dawes
intends to sell the personal financial information
of government employees to "the Russian,"
OMEGA engages undercover agent Cutter Smith.
Tailing her all the way to France, Cutter is
fighting a growing attraction to Mallory while at
the same time having to determine her connection
to "the Russian." Is Mallory really the mouse in
this game of cat and mouse?

Look for

Stranded with a Spy

by *USA TODAY* bestselling author
Merline Lovelace

October 2007.

Also available October wherever you buy books:

BULLETPROOF MARRIAGE *(Mission: Impassioned)*
by Karen Whiddon

A HERO'S REDEMPTION *(Haven)* by Suzanne McMinn

TOUCHED BY FIRE by Elizabeth Sinclair

Welcome to our newest miniseries, about five
poker players and the women who love them!

Texas Hold'em

When it comes to love, the stakes are high

Beginning October 2007 with

THE BABY GAMBLE

by USA TODAY *bestselling author*

Tara Taylor Quinn

#1446

Desperate to have a baby, Annie Kincaid
turns to the only man she trusts, her ex-husband,
Blake Smith, and asks him to father her child.

Also watch for:

REQUEST YOUR FREE BOOKS!
2 FREE NOVELS PLUS 2
FREE GIFTS!

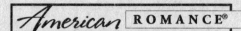

Heart, Home & Happiness!

Harlequin® Historical
Historical Romantic Adventure!

A WESTERN WINTER WONDERLAND

with three fantastic stories
by
Cheryl St.John,
Jenna Kernan
and ## Pam Crooks

Don't miss these three
unforgettable stories about
the struggles of the Wild West
and the strong women who
find love and happiness
on Christmas Day.

Look for
A WESTERN WINTER
WONDERLAND

*Available October
wherever you buy books.*

Silhouette®

Desire

There was only one man for the job—
an impossible-to-resist maverick
she knew she didn't dare fall for.

MAVERICK
(#1827)

BY *NEW YORK TIMES*
BESTSELLING AUTHOR
JOAN HOHL

"Will You Do It for One Million Dollars?"

Any other time, Tanner Wolfe would have balked at being
hired by a woman. Yet Brianna Stewart was desperate to
engage the infamous bounty hunter. The price was just
high enough to gain Tanner's interest…Brianna's beauty
definitely strong enough to keep it. But he wasn't about
to allow her to tag along on his mission. He worked
alone. Always had. Always would. However, he'd never
confronted a more determined client than Brianna. She
wasn't taking no for an answer—not about anything.

Perhaps a million-dollar bounty was not the only thing
this maverick was about to gain….

Look for MAVERICK

Available October 2007 wherever you buy books.